BLACK GIGOLO 2
(Vrais Jumeaux)

A Novel

DENZIL DEVARRO

DEDICATION

This book is dedicated to my four family members that have passed in the last 18 months. First of all my niece sweet Charlisa Smith, my beautiful sister Cheryl Ann Andrews, my go-getter sister Joyce Elaine Andrews and my sister who took no stuff from anybody Erica Elise Andrews. This last year and a half has been a nightmare for me and my family but we must move on and continue to live and have faith that all things happen for a reason.

If You Believe

Men have turned their back on love
They say it's a word that has no meaning
They say there's no faith, no God above
To even believe can really seem demeaning
But I say hold on to your dreams
Cause if you don't you'll be deceived
You can overcome the world and its schemes
If only brother you continue to believe

Sometimes you're degraded and then knocked down
And you think that you're not a part of the plan
Just hold your head up it will all turn around
It's a beautiful thing just to be a man
There are times when you can't sleep at night

And you wake up in fear not knowing what to do
You must live by faith and not by sight
The most beautiful thing is just being you

From Malcolm X to Martin Luther King
Powerful men have spoken from the heart
If we believe in each other we all can sing
And nothing in the world can tear us apart
A mask can't hide the pain I feel
A virus can't keep me from being strong
The vaccine of love is the only thing that heals
If we stand together we can never go wrong

There once was a time when I was afraid
And I did not want to come outside
I felt that my life was just a masquerade
I would just lay in my room and hide
But then I started to have faith in me
And then my blessings I started to receive
I opened my eyes and I started to see
And it all happened when I started to believe

— Denzil Devarro

CHAPTER 1

MY NOSY NEIGHBOR

It's noon on a Friday in Los Angeles, CA and Michael Alexander is relaxing in his rented ranch-style cottage on Magnolia Street in North Hollywood, a fairly upscale suburb of Los Angeles. Michael is putting together some numbers for his 3 pm showing that he has with a client by the name of Darlene Orbison, a recent divorcee who is independently wealthy and looking to start a new life after five years of marriage. Michael is making a few calls to get all his "ducks in a row" before leaving. He first calls Darlene Orbison to verify their appointment.

"Mrs. Orbison," says Michael. "Is it Mrs. or Ms"?

"It's Ms. I dropped my "slave" name as soon as the divorce was final."

"Okay Ms. Orbison," I'm just calling to confirm our 3 o'clock appointment at the house in Sherman Oaks, you're going to love this house, it's perfect for someone such as yourself looking to start over. Now I think you told me that you didn't have any children."

"Thank God no," says Ms. Orbison, "I don't have any attachments to that man. It was hard enough getting away from that man by myself, having kids would have been a nightmare."

"Alright, Ms. Orbison," says Michael. "I will see you at 3 pm and I look forward to meeting you, bye now." Michael hangs up the phone and calls the car dealership where his car is being serviced. A man answers the phone and Michael begins to speak.

"Yea hello, my name is Michael Alexander and I'm calling to see if my car will be ready soon because I have a 3 o'clock appointment that I can't miss.

"Let me check". After holding on for three minutes the man finally returns to the phone.

"Mr. Alexander," says the man, "We have had a bit of a problem with your vehicle."

"What kind of a problem"? asks Michael.

"The Mercedes dealership did not have the part we needed in stock, so they had to order it and we won't receive it until about 2 pm so your car won't be ready before 5 pm."

"5," replies Michael, "I made sure I explained to them when I brought the car in that I had to have the car back no later than 2 pm. I have a very important appointment at 3 pm today that I can't be late for.

"I am very sorry Mr. Alexander," replies the man, "I will discount the service another 20 percent and I will have the car dropped off at your home to spare you the inconvenience of having to pick it up but this could not be avoided, sir. In order to ensure the quality of work that we have come to be known for, we need that final part." "Inconvenience," says Michael. "How about the inconvenience of not making your first solo appointment." Michael would normally have a shouting session with the employee but he is trying to turn over a "new leaf". Michael wanted his new convertible Mercedes in the parking lot when his client showed up to set the mood, but he took it in stride.

"Okay," says Michael. "I guess I'll just take an Uber." He ends his call with the employee and calls his friend Eric Means.

"Eric," says Michael. "What up home team."

"I'm rolling right now brother," says Eric. "What's the deallyo good brother?"

"I need a lift, my brother," says Michael. "I got my first solo at 3 o'clock but the Mercedes dealership won't have my car ready til five my boy." Eric Means is a light-complexioned black man that also works in the Real Estate game although at a different company from Michael. Eric stands about 6 ft 2 inches tall with a low haircut and a somewhat muscular build from Carson, CA, another suburb of Los Angeles. Eric and Michael are the best of friends and call on each other for any and everything.

"Can't do it brother," states Eric, "Moms needs me at 2. Take an Uber over there and I will meet you there at 3 after I finish with mom. I will drive my Benz over because knowing you all you are looking for is the ambiance."

"Yea brother," replies Michael, "got to set that trap brother. First impressions are the most important." "Agreed," says Eric, "text me the address and I will be there by no later than 2:45 after I finish up with Mom's, what you "sporting" over there."

"I'm wearing the" killer" corporate America blue suit with the tie the same color as the suit. She ain't gonna know what hit her," states Michael. "Be careful, '' says Eric, "don't get too sharp, she might want to buy more than the house."

"No more of that brother," says Michael. "I'm moving on up and Real Estate is the only thing I got for sale. I'll text you the address, I got to start getting ready since "my boy" made me take an Uber. I'm gonna "member" this."

"Come on brother with your "Bougie" ass," says Eric, "it won't kill you to take an Uber for once. Besides, I'm glad you're not driving because afterward I want to take you to this new spot in Long Beach. Steve says the girls are to die for brother."

"Steve," says Michael. "Steve wouldn't know a fine woman if she bit him on the ass. His last girl was so ugly his dog wouldn't even play with her, and she was fat. The last time we went out with Steve the tab was over $200 and most of that was food for his girl."

"Just because he likes big women doesn't mean he doesn't know a fine woman when he sees one," states Eric, "anyway I gotta go brother, text me the address and I will see you there at 2:45 and, enjoy that Uber ride brother."

"Funny," says Michael. "Later." Michael hangs up the call and checks the clock to see that it is already after 1 o'clock and he jumps in the shower and starts to get ready. He is very deliberate when he dresses so he knows he needs plenty of time to get ready and he needs the Uber to be there no later than 2. After a nice shower, Michael puts on his 40 dollar silk underwear and his wife-beater tee shirt.

"Expensive draws," says Michael to himself. He throws on the blue Kenneth Cole suit with the blue tie to match with the stretchy white Mizzen and Main shirt and the blue Ferragamo boots. Michael checks himself out in the mirror and compliments himself.

"I'm so pretty I would date myself if I could," says Michael as he checks the time on his watch and realizes it is almost 2, "Ah shit, I better call this Uber and get out of here." He calls the Uber and grabs his briefcase with all the documents he thinks he will need and as he retrieves everything as the Uber driver pulls up. Outside Michael's nosy, elderly white neighbor makes an observation.

"I guess you finally wrecked that nice car," states Michael's neighbor Mrs. Crabbs," as fast as you drive I knew it would only be a matter of time."

"I'm having service done Mrs. Crabbs," says Michael. "It will be here later." As Michael jumps in the Uber driver's truck Mrs. Crabbs keeps talking. "What kind of service and where are you off to now?" asks Mrs. Crabbs.

"None of your business Mrs. Crabbs," yells Michael, "why don't you go in your house and brush your false teeth or something and get you some business of your own." As the Uber driver takes off Mrs. Crabbs is still talking.

"I will have you know that these are my real teeth," she whispers.

"Nosy Bitch," says Michael under his breath.

CHAPTER 2

A TERRIFIED BUYER

Michael looks over his notes and at about 2:40 he pulls up to the Sherman Oaks address and finds his friend Eric already parked in the yard. Michael acknowledges the Uber driver and adds a $15 tip to the app for the driver and exits the car.

"Thank you sir," says Michael. "I'm going to give you a very good review." Eric exits the car and the two men acknowledge each other.

"Eric, my boy," yells Michael, "good looking out baby boy. I can always count on you." The two men give each other a cordial embrace as Michael prepares for his first solo showing.

"You know I wouldn't ever let you down brother," says Eric," I'll just sit in the car and let you do your thang. I'll get in the passenger seat and crouch down and even if she does see me sitting on the passenger side she will think the car is yours." "Good looking out brother," says Michael. "I better get inside in case she arrives early."

"Digging that suit brother," says Eric, "a lot of Bro's rocking them skinny suits nowadays, I guess I better get with the times." Eric has a very muscular frame packing 230 pounds of his muscle on his body with a slight "gut".

"Get you one brother," says Michael facetiously, not believing what he says, "you will probably wear it well." Michael runs to the lock box and opens the house as Eric gets in the car on the passenger side. He knows the layout of the home and works on his spiel and at 2:55 he looks out the window and sees a white Land Rover pulling in the driveway. He checks all things involving the house as Eric looks out the car window and sees the gorgeous Darlene Orbison, a woman of Armenian descent that looks white to Eric. Eric texts Michael as he sits low in the passenger seat.

"Michael," texts Eric, "Man wait 'til you see how fine this white girl is. She got some black in her somewhere. If not, I would sure like to give her some black." Michael looks out the window and just says "wow". Michael texts Eric back.

"You ain't "shitting" she is fine, "man what a body. I don't remember the last time I saw a white girl that fine." Michael finishes his text and runs upstairs quickly to take his briefcase as Ms. Orbison heads for the door and she simply opens it and lets herself in.

"Mr. Alexander," says Ms. Orbison, "Are you here sir?"

"Yes ma'am," says Michael. "Coming down now, had to put something upstairs." As Michael slowly walks downstairs Ms. Orbison heads straight for the kitchen and checks out the decor of the home.

"Oh this is Nice," says Ms. Orbison, "I can see myself cozying up in this living room with that fireplace and I love that marble island in this kitchen." As Ms. Orbison heads for the kitchen Michael approaches her from behind and begins to introduce himself.

"Hi Ms. Orbison," says Michael as Ms. Orbison still has her back turned. "It's nice to finally put a name with a face." Ms. Orbison turns around to acknowledge Michael and takes one look at him and freezes in terror and her eyes bulge out while she stares.

"You," says Ms. Orbison. "You, you." Ms. Orbison lets out a blood curdling scream and runs right past Michael and dashes out the door screaming in terror and losing one of her heels as she falls down in the yard while looking back at Michael as he stands in the doorway in confusion.

"Ms. Orbison, what's wrong," yells Michael as the woman screams and cries in terror and fumbles with her keys as she tries to use her fob to open the car. Eric emerges from the car and the woman gets even more terrified as she sees him. Michael walks towards the car wondering what is wrong as Ms. Orbison jumps in the car and speeds out of the driveway. Michael approaches Eric who has his mouth open in amazement.

"Man what did you do?" asks Eric. "I don't think I have ever seen anyone that terrified before."

"I didn't do anything," answered Michael, "I reached out my hand to introduce myself and she just started screaming. She kept saying you, you or something like that. Her eyes man, something is wrong with that lady man."

"Maybe she didn't like the wallpaper," jokes Eric. "You should tell her we can have that fixed.

"Let's go brother," says Eric. "A screaming white woman and two brothers is the recipe for disaster."

"We didn't do anything wrong," says Michael. "Why should we run."

"We don't have to do anything wrong brother," says Eric, "You know how it works."

Michaels thinks for a second and comes to his senses. "Just let me close this lockbox." He closes the lockbox and he and Eric take off and about 3 miles up the road they pass about 7 police cars going in the direction of the house.

"I wonder where they headed?" asks Michael jokingly. "Maybe they headed for the house after us."

"That's not funny," says Eric.

CHAPTER 3

SCENE OF THE CRIME

The men continue to drive and sure enough the police cars pull up to the house where Michael was and pull out their guns and they immediately call the homeowner to get the lockbox code and go inside with guns drawn and clear the house. As the police clear the house they look around for anything that might catch their eye and give them a clue to what might have gone on. Detective Sergeant Dwayne Hall is assigned to the scene and looks through the house as he talks to the Sherman Oaks police officers.

"Nothing seems out of place Sergeant," says one police officer. "Nothing but balloons and water and all kinds of goodies, the house is immaculate." "The woman sounded terrified to the operator," says Sergeant Hall, "She says one or two men was trying to rape her."

"No Sergeant," says a police officer. "She said one of the men did rape her."

"But where," says Sergeant Hall. "Nothing seems even slightly out of place. I wish my house was this clean." A police officer comes walking slowly from upstairs holding a nice leather briefcase. "Found this upstairs sir," says the officer as he gives Sergeant Hall the bag.

"Nice bag," says Sergeant Hall, "Upfront Realty." "That's a big company," says one of the officers. "And we got a name," says Sergeant Hall., "Michael Alexander. Alexander, Alexander. Why does that name sound familiar?"

"I don't know sir," says an officer. "Maybe he is the one who was showing her the house."

"Ms. Orbison," says an officer, "the lady who made the complaint, went straight to the precinct. They say she is hysterical."

"Ok," says Sergeant Hall, "I am going to have a talk with her, you boys keep looking and let me know if you find anything." The Sergeant pulls one of the Detectives to the side, "get me a read on Upfront Realty and find out anything you can about this Michael Alexander. I don't see any crime committed here but something scared the hell out of that lady so I'm going to talk to her."

Meanwhile, back in the car Michael has a realization.

CHAPTER 4

LOOKING TO UNWIND

"Damn man," says Michael. "I left my briefcase at that house."

"So what," says Eric.

"So what," replies Michael, "all my personal and business information is in there."

"So," says Eric, "there is a lock box on the house and you would have to know the code to get in. Pick it up in the morning when you get your car. Let's hit the spot in Long Beach, we can get there by 5 and happy hour will just be kicking off. Let me buy you a couple of drinks to get that psycho "bitch" buyer out of your mind. Steve will be there and he can introduce us to some of his girls that he knows from the spot."

"No way," says Michael. "I don't want to meet any women Steve knows, at least not without a harpoon."

"Man you better stop talking about people like that," says Eric, "and for the record, I wonder what was up with that chick at that house, man whatever she was scared of, it was real. You sure you have never met that woman before?"

"Man I told you," says Michael. "I have never seen that chick before in my life. I am just as confused as you. By the way, what's the name of this spot we are going to in Long Beach?"

"It's called Black Long Beach, '' says Eric. "The food is good, the women are fine and they make real good drinks which I'm sure you need. The same people I believe own that spot also own Black Hollywood and you know how that spot is popping. You need to get your mind off your troubles, everything happens for a reason my brother although I must admit that I can't rationalize what we just went through and what it could mean. Sit back and chill and leave the driving to me."

"I need to call the car dealership and tell them to just keep my car until tomorrow," says Michael. "'I will just pick it up myself. My nosy neighbor Mrs. Crabbs will be all in my business if I am not there when they deliver it today. I think that old buzzard has "crabs."

"You know you hit that man," says Eric, "her husband gonna whup your ass. How good is that old white coochie brother?"

"You tell me," says Michael. "That's why you hang around the area when I'm not there. I knew you had secrets."

"Whatever," says Eric, "I wouldn't hit that with your dick." Michael and Eric both laugh.

CHAPTER 5

A WOMAN TERRIFIED

As Michael and Eric head towards Black Long Beach, Detective Hall arrives back at The Sherman Oaks police station and he is immediately confronted by an older black female Detective Lieutenant Jocelyn Towns, a 20 year veteran of the LA police department who has conducted the interview with Ms. Orbison so far. "What have you got," says Sergeant Hall, did we do a rape kit on the woman, are there scratches, bruises, anything."

"Nothing," says Lieutenant Towns. "She's incoherent, she seems terrified. Yet there are no signs of a struggle, no marks, no bruises and definitely no semen of any kind or any other bodily fluids. I think the woman has lost it, maybe we should call detox and turn her over to psych because she is tripping hard off of something." Sergeant Hall looks through the mirror at the terrified woman and agrees with Lieutenant Towns but he wants to question the woman himself.

"Give me a few minutes with her Lieutenant Towns," states Sergeant Hall, "what do we have to lose?"

Another plainclothes Officer comes out of the back and starts to speak to Sergeant Hall. "Sergeant Hall," states the officer, " I've got some information on our victim."

"What you got," asks Sergeant Hall.

"Well her last name is Orbison now but it was Peterson up until 6 months ago," says the detective, "she is a recent divorcee. And get this, 6 months ago she was brutally raped and sodomized and she spent several weeks in the hospital. The perpetrator did everything but kill her. I also have the information on that Realtor who left the bag at the house, Michael Alexander, turns out he was involved with a woman named Coretta James, and get this, he was a male prostitute."

"They are called Gigolos," says Sergeant Hall," now that's what I call a major career change from Gigolo to Realtor."

"Yeah," says the Detective, "it seems he moved to Alabama for a while and he's been back here a few years and he has kept himself totally under the radar, not even a parking ticket. He lives in North Hollywood off Magnolia in a cottage. He's got a 10 year old daughter and seems to live a very quiet life, he went from a Gigolo to a square, a real L7."

"Ok, send some guys over there to talk to Mr. Alexander the ex Gigolo," says Sergeant Hall "while I talk to Ms. Orbison and see what I can get out of her."

CHAPTER 6

ALL EYES ON ME

While all that is going on at the Sherman Oaks police station, Michael Alexander and Eric Means pull up to the front of the club called Black Long Beach where they see their friend Steve waiting for them near the entrance.

"Stevie boy," yells Eric, "good to see you man." Eric and Steve embrace and Michael also embraces Steve.

"Where big um," says Michael referring to Steve's girl that he thinks is fat, "if she's inside you better tell the maître d' to order up a truck load of wings for an appetizer."

"Man you better leave my woman alone," says Steve, "I can't help it you like those anorexic women. I like my women to have some meat on their bones."

"Well you succeeded in that brother," says Michael. "I saw hippos that didn't have that much meat on their bones." Steve is 6ft tall and 200 lbs with medium complexion and curly hair and a very jovial character that loves to joke and have fun. As the three men laugh and joke with each other Michael notices a man staring very intently at him from a distance. After he continues to stare, Michael brings it to the attention of his friends.

"Hey man," says Michael. "Look at big brother over there staring at me." The man starts to speak to Michael from a distance.

"Marvin," says the man, 'Marvin Williams, where you've been hiding man?"

"You're talking to me?" asks Michael.

"Yea I'm talking to you Marvin," says the man. "You never paid me for that package you got from me and I want my money." Steve and Eric look at the man and look back at Michael not knowing what to think.

"Man you got me confused with somebody," states Michael, "my name is not Marvin it's Michael and I never saw you before in my life." Michael gestures to Steve and Eric" come on brothers let's go inside" as the man continues to stare at him with a menacing look.

"I want my money Marvin," yells the man as Michael and his friends enter Black Long Beach.

The club has a modern deco design with pictures of black entertainers and athletes on the wall along with a very comfortable seating. There is a large outdoor patio, a fireplace inside the lounge and another portion of the bar in the back containing a humidor with the finest cigars for those who like to smoke "stogies".

"Man this is hip," says Michael. "This is my kind of spot." Eric and Steve are still a little shaken by what just happened outside and Eric can't forget the incident from earlier.

"That's twice in one day," says Eric.

"What do you mean twice?" asks Steve. Eric looks at Michael and waits for a response.

"Ok," says Michael. "When I was showing the house the client just freaks out when she sees me and starts screaming and running out the door and takes off out of the driveway like a bat out of hell and she was so frantic that she almost ran off the road. And I can't be sure but I think she called the police cause Eric and I passed a shit load of police headed in the direction of the house." "What did she say to you when she saw you Michael"? asks Steve.

"She just stared at me," says Michael. "I could see in her eyes she was terrified and she kept saying, you, you, you and then she ran out of the house screaming."

"You know her?," asks Steve.

"Hell no," says Michael. "I've never seen that woman before in my life."

"Sad too," says Eric, "'cause she was fine as hell." "Come on man," Steve says, putting his arm around Michael. "Let me buy you a drink. Sounds like you need one." As the three guys walk to the seating area Steve notices a heavy set, attractive Black women looking at him from a distance and Michael notices.

"Man I'm not paying another $200 dollar food tab," says Michael sarcastically, "you on your own this time." As the three men walk towards their seating area Eric notices that several of the patrons and members of the wait staff are staring intently at them and Eric begins to feel quite uncomfortable.

"Is it just me or does it feel like we're being watched?" asks Eric, "all eyes on us."

"Well what do you expect brother?" asks Michael. "We are the three smoothest brothers in here, even when we got Steve we are still smooth."

"Fuck you," says Steve to Michael. With it being a sunny day the three sit themselves on the outdoor patio and expect to be approached by a member of the wait staff but no one comes to serve them and the wait staff just stands around talking to each other while they continue to stare at Michael.

"Man this is a nice spot but they got some terrible service," yells Steve, "I'm just going to go to the bar and get a couple of drinks. What y'all drinking?"

"I'll take a brew," says Eric, "a Corona."

"Hey man give me a double shot of that Balvenie," says Michael. "I need a pick me up."

"I hope that picks you up," says Steve "that's the highest priced shit in the bar." Steve heads for the bar while Michael just relaxes and enjoys the evening and Eric continues to look around at the various eyes fixated at their table.

"Relax brother," says Michael to a paranoid Eric, "tune out whatever it is that is bothering you." While Eric stresses at the prying eyes inside the bar outside, the man that confronted Michael waits intently in his car for Michael to leave the restaurant, packing a long handled silver 357 magnum with hollow point bullets.

As Steve approaches the bartender he tries his normal jovial approach but finds that the bartender is not in the mood.

"Tighten my drink up real good because I'm a big time tipper," jokes Steve, "I've put some kids through college with my tips." The bartender just frowns at Steve and makes a derogatory comment while pointing at Michael.

"Be careful of the company you keep," says the bartender, "you lay down with dogs you wake up with fleas."

"Yea," says Steve with a moan, "thanks for the life lesson. Can I get a Long Island Iced Tea, a Corona, and..." As Steve tries to continue his order the Bartender cuts him short.

"And let me guess," says the Bartender, a double shot of Balvenie." Steve just looks at the Bartender and acknowledges the Balvenie order as the bartender reluctantly prepares the drinks and when she turns to pour the Balvenie she spits in Michael's drink and stirs it into the drink. Steve offers up his card for the transaction and adds a $20 tip and heads back towards the table.

"Tell Steve to put my drink on the table and I will be right back," says Michael," I'm going on the Cigar side and grab me one of those "stogies". Michael leaves the table and walks through the doors where the Humidor is set up so that he can grab his own cigar. As Michael walks away Steve returns with the drinks and seems a little shaken.

"You alright?" asks Eric. "You look like you saw a ghost."

"There's something strange going on in here," says Steve, "everybody watching us and especially Mike. You sure he has never been here before?"

"That's what he told me," says Eric, "but from the vibe I'm getting he seems well known. And I just looked outside and that guy that confronted him when we came in is still there waiting in his car, if you look across you can see him sitting there. And he got something shiny in his hand.

"You think it is a gun?" asks Steve, "man what's going on."

"I'm sure it's a gun," says Eric, "and that brother looks like he means business." As Steve and Eric talk, Michael walks into the cigar room and notices all eyes on him. Michael looks through the cigar selection as a man seems to be standing over him watching his every move.

"Can I help you with something?" asks Michael. "Any particular reason you are standing over me?" "Hurry up," says the man, "make your selection and get out of here."

"If you don't stop standing over me I'm gonna hurry up and put something on your ass," says Michael. The attendant gestures the man away from Michael and speaks his mind.

"We don't want any more trouble like the last time," says the Attendant, "just get your cigar and move on." Michael grabs a $20 Oliva cigar and pulls out his card to pay.

"Cash only," says the Attendant, "we only accept cash." Michael looks over to the other counters and notices several people paying with their cards and he realizes that the cash only rule is intended for him. He again notices all eyes on him and reaches in his pocket and finds a $20 bill and a $5 dollar bill.

"This should cover it," says Michael as he hands the man the money. The man keeps the money and throws Michaels $5 dollar bill on the ground. "I don't want a tip from you," says the man," take your $5 and stick it up your ass." Michael frowns at the man and makes a gesture but wisely realizes he is not wanted in the room so he slowly walks out and back into the main room where all eyes focus. He takes a look down at his drink and sees something floating on top as his two friends also wonder what is going on. The owner of the establishment comes over towards Michael's table and speaks to him and his friends.

"Sir, as the owner of this establishment I can refuse to provide service to anyone and because of your actions on the last occasion that you were here we can no longer serve you," says the owner, "so finish your drink and leave immediately." Michael stares at the drink with the spit floating on top and has a bewildered look on his face.

"May I ask why you are asking me to leave"? inquires Michael. The owner gives Michael a sarcastic look and reaches in his pocket and pulls out a long receipt and shows it to Michael. He looks at the bottoms of the receipt and sees a bill for $2300. Michael looks at the bill and sees food and champagne and cigars and all sorts of large orders.

"You see Mr. Williams, we don't like dead beats in here," says the owner, "my waiter still is in the hospital recovering from that beating you gave him. Not only do we want you to leave now but we never want to see you in here again. Now get out." Steve and Eric start to move towards the door but Michael stubbornly speaks back.

"I've got to take a leak," says Michael sarcastically, "be right back."

CHAPTER 7

THE GREAT ESCAPE

Michael slowly walks towards the bathroom and unbeknownst to him a large dark skinned male follows him into the restroom. While Michael heads towards the restroom Eric and Steve remain terrified by the crowd. Michael enters the restroom and closes the stall and he hears the door open behind him and he hears footsteps come in behind him. He realizes he has nowhere to run and he urinates and takes his time coming out. The footsteps seem to have stopped moving right in front of the bathroom stall and Michael slowly opens the bathroom stall to see a large black male standing by the door.

"Where's my sister?" says the man, "she left with you the other night and no one has seen her since."

"What's your sisters name?" asks Michael.

"You know her name nigga, Tina Randolph, what did you do to her?" asks the man.

"Brother, as God is my witness I've never met your sister," says Michael. "Now step aside so I can get out of here."

"The only way you get out of this bathroom," says the man as he pops open a switchblade knife, "is over my dead body. Where is Tina at fool?"

"Man I told you I don't know no damn Tina," says Michael. "You better step your ugly ass aside." As the guy starts to lunge with the knife Michael remembers that he had not finished urinating in the toilet and he pulls his penis and begins to urinate on the man's shoes."

"You nasty motherfucker," says the man. The man starts to come forward but loses his balance as he slips in the urine but he swings the knife several times at Michael and cuts him across the shoulder.

"Ah," yells Michael as he is cut. As the man lunges for Michael again he slips a little and as he falls forward Michael slams his head into the bathroom stall and as he falls to the floor Michael runs from the bathroom full speed. As Michael exits the bathroom he notices Steve and Eric have exited the restaurant and he is all on his own. Michael runs from the restaurant and the man that was waiting for him with a gun is no longer waiting in front of the club. As Michael starts to run away from the club Eric pulls up out of nowhere.

"Get in man," yells Eric, "let's get the fuck out of here." Eric speeds off down the 91 freeway with Michael barely making it into the car and the stunned man with the gun outside the club pulls back up and looks on from a distance as Michael and Eric speed down the freeway.

"Wow," says Michael. "That was some intense shit." Eric gives Michael a piercing glaze.

"Alright Michael," says Eric, "what the fuck is going on, and how did you get that cut."

"A man came behind me into the bathroom and he said I left out with his sister the other night and nobody has seen her since," says Michael. "He cut me with a switchblade knife."

"That shit looks like it hurts," says Eric as Michael bleeds from his shoulder," we better get you to a hospital."

"It's not that bad," says Michael. "Just a flesh wound. The man couldn't get his balance when he was trying to stab me and he fell forward. I slammed his head into the bathroom wall."

"Wonder why he slipped?" asks Eric. "I guess it doesn't matter as long as you got out safely. Nasty ass restaurant, talking all that shit and can't clean up a pissy bathroom."

"Yeah," says Michael. "That was a pissy situation." "Mike," says Eric, "they accusing you of some serious stuff, "they say you ran up a $2000 tab, you was talking loud and cussing out the patrons and that you left with some girl that didn't come back and she hasn't been seen since. What's up brother."

"No idea," says Michael," but I know one thing, I'm going to find out what just happened. I still need me a drink, this has been the day from hell."

"You must be reading my mind brother," says Eric," we're gonna meet that boy Steve at a hole in the wall in South Central, we're gonna throw a few back and chalk this up to a real bad day. You know Michael, they say everybody out there has somebody that looks like them, your alter ego sounds like a lunatic."

"I thought Steve bailed on me," says Michael. "I wouldn't have blamed him."

"Naw man," says Eric, "he helped me pull the 'okey doke' on that guy waiting in the front for you to come out. Michael, you my boy and I love you like a brother, but something serious is going on in your life and you need to find out what it is before somebody tries to put you six feet deep."

"No diggity," says Michael.

CHAPTER 8

SORTING OUT A CRIME

Michael and Eric make a b-line towards the 'hole in the wall' club in South Central while back in the SOPD precinct Lieutenant Towns and Sergeant Hall try to talk to the incoherent Ms. Orbison who is still very erratic. Lieutenant Towns brings in a bottle of water and puts her arms around the victim while Sergeant Hall tries to get some information out of the terrified woman.

"Ms. Orbison," says Sergeant Hall, "are you saying that a rape occurred today while you were looking to purchase that house, because ma'am I have to say that we went over that house with a fine tooth comb and the spot is so clean that you can eat off the floor. We found nothing."

"No, you idiot," yells Ms. Orbison, "he raped me six months ago. He stuck a bottle in my vagina. Then he put a plastic bag over my face and pulled it until I almost stopped breathing. Then he let go of the bag and while I was gagging and gasping for my breath he started pulling my hair, and he said and I quote "bitches like to have your hair pulled while you're fucking." Ms. Orbison pauses while tears stream down her eyes.

"He snatched a big part out of the front of my hair," says Ms. Orbison. Orbison takes her hand off the water bottle and pulls off the wig she is wearing and reveals a large bald spot in the front of her hair. The two police officers gasp in horror at the site of the woman with a large part of her scalp missing.

"You know what I can't do," states Ms. Orbison matter of factly, "I can't have any children, I can't have sex, hell, I don't even want a man to touch me, to look at me, my husband left me, I was so messed up that I have had over ten surgeries, people look at me differently, they all say 'I'm so sorry' and as soon as I walk away I hear the whispers behind my back. And then today I see that fucking "animal" and all the memories and the pain came rushing back. I go home every night not knowing if I am going to kill myself, not knowing if I did something to deserve this, I don't even consider myself a human being. And today, the pain starts all over again." For a few moments there is complete silence in the room. Lieutenant Towns hugs the woman and assures her that she deserves to live.

"You didn't do anything wrong honey," says Lieutenant Towns. "I know I can't feel what you feel right now but I promise you we will get this moron, we're gonna get him. We know where he lives and we'll get him." Sergeant Hall stands up and rubs the woman on her shoulder and just walks out of the room. He walks into the hallway and holds his head down and visualizes the story that Ms. Orbison had just told him. Lieutenant Towns exits the room for a moment to speak to Sergeant Hall.

"Get that sick motherfucker," says Lieutenant Towns. "We gotta get him off the streets before he does this to someone else."

"There ain't no telling how many people he has already done it to." Get the swat team out there to his house and put out a BOLO on this bastard." "The BOLO is already out and we have officers already watching his house waiting for his return and they are going through his garbage to get his DNA and after we get verification of his DNA sample then we will get the SWAT team out there to get his ass," says Sergeant Hall.

"What are we waiting for," says Lieutenant Towns. "You heard what she said he did to her."

"If we arrest him without proper verification of the evidence, that fool might walk. I want his ass and I am going to dot every I and cross every T, he ain't getting away. Don't worry, his ass is grass and you are looking at the lawnmower."

CHAPTER 9

THE STAKEOUT BEGINS

Back at Michael's home a police car is parked out front and Mrs. Crabbs comes out of her home as the police go back and forth through Michael's empty garbage.

"Are you men looking for Michael," asks Mrs. Crabbs, "I knew someone would come looking for him eventually. He always got women in and out of here and different people coming through. Are you the police" The plainclothes officer asks Mrs. Crabbs some questions.

"Do you know where Mr. Alexander is right now," asks the officer.

"He took an Uber out at 2:50 today and I think he was going to show a house," says Ms. Crabbs, "I'm the President of the neighborhood watch and I try to make sure that things go correctly in the neighborhood. I think he smokes weed daily and he's got a lot going on. He is just not good for the neighborhood, there's a bunch of elderly people living around here and we don't need this constant activity." Mrs. Crabbs is talking so much that the officer has to stop her from talking.

"Thank you Mrs. Craft," says the officer.

"That's Crabbs," she says, "Susan Crabbs, I was a model at one time but I had to give it up because I got pregnant and my husband didn't want me to be in that game. Michael doesn't even look at me, he thinks he is better than the rest of us". The officer looks at the 60ish, heavy set white woman and hands her a card.

"Thank you Mrs. Crabbs and if we need any more information from you we will get in touch with you and if you think of anything useful, please give us a call." Mrs. Crabbs still talks and mumbles as the officer continues to look around the property.

"By the way," says Mrs. Crabbs. "Garbage day is tomorrow. Michael usually puts his garbage out the morning of."

While this exchange is going on Sergeant Hall is seeking an order to search Michael's residence and also an order to obtain his DNA to test against the sample left behind when Ms. Orbison was raped and sodomized six months earlier. They also plan on testing Michael's DNA against several unsolved rapes including two incidents where the victims were also killed. With it being so late in the evening the officer expects the order to be signed in the morning. Until then all they can do is wait.

CHAPTER 10

THE HOLE IN THE WALL

At about 8pm Michael and Eric pull up to The Hole in The Wall club that is actually called The Hole in The Wall.

"The name of this shit is really The Hole in The Wall?" asks Michael. "What's it like in there?"

"It's nice in there," says Eric, "a little different clientele though, they let their hair down in here brother, no bougie LA shit."

"Any fine women?" asks Michael.

"You tell me," answers Eric pointing to two beautiful black women and a gorgeous woman of Spanish descent walking into the club and other women coming.

"Ah yeah, here we go," yells Michael, "what we waiting on, let's get in there."

"Hold on, yells Eric pulling a blunt from his pocket, hit this with me, this will calm you down after the day you had."

"When you started smoking weed?" asks Michael.

"I always have," says Eric, "but I don't do it all the time and I don't let anybody know that I do it, I don't tell everybody my business."

"Man I haven't smoked weed in 5 years," says Michael. "That shit might take me way over the top."

"Just take a toke," says Eric while lighting up the weed and taking a toke himself. Eric starts to cough as he passes the blunt to Michael. Michael just stares at the weed as if he has seen a ghost.

"Go head man," says Eric, that will calm you down and relax you." Michael takes a toke and handles it well and then takes another toke.

"Aight, that's enough," says Eric, "this the sticky icky icky, you don't want to hit that too hard. Alright let's get in here and get at it. Steve should already be in here." Michael and Eric exit the car and after being patted down at the door by the bouncer they enter The Hole in The Wall. The club has a very spacious layout with a much more casual setting and decor, there are tables for large parties and several sofas for those who want a more intimate feel. The music is more "old school" and it has a large dance floor that is full of people. It's open Mic night so at 9 o'clock the DJ will open the club to anyone who wants to perform in any way. Michael sees a few women making eye contact with him as soon as he walks in.

"These chicks real friendly at this spot huh," says Michael. "I see a bunch of them checking me out already."

"Yeah brother," says Eric,"these women over here are about it. They are fine, they are beautiful and extremely friendly. This is the spot you come to when you want to have a good time, judgment free." As Michael and Eric talk a beautiful server starts to speak to him.

"Excuse me sir," says the server to Michael, "you see that you lady over there at that table to the left, she would like to buy you a drink." Michael looks over to the table and acknowledges the very attractive black female.

"I'll take a scotch," says Michael. "Neat, that means no ice."

"I wasn't born under a rock," says Eric, "I know what neat means."

"I'll be back brother," says Michael.

"I'll have a scotch also," says Eric to the server as Michael walks off. Michael approaches the table where three beautiful black women are seated.

"Thank you so much for the drink," says Michael as he reaches for the woman's outreached hand. My name is Michael Alexander and it's always a pleasure to see beautiful black women."

"You're pretty easy on the eyes yourself," says the woman, "my name is Erica Elise, and these are my girls Sharon and Jamie."

The two women acknowledge Michael.

"The pleasure is all mine ladies and I hope it will be okay Ms. Elise if I come back over and ask for a dance."

"Who's your friend," asks Jamie.

"Oh that's my boy Eric," says Michael. As Michael speaks he notices a woman from across the bar staring at him, a woman that looks somewhat familiar to him. His staring is noticed by the women.

"Don't you think it's kind of rude to stare," asks Sharon, "especially while you are talking to other people."

"I'm very sorry ladies, I didn't mean to be rude," says Michael.

"But you were," snaps Sharon, "brothers just ain't gonna do right." Michael starts to snap back but he simply thanks Ms. Elise again and moves on. Eric approaches Michael with his drink.

"Here's your drink brother," says Eric, "don't get caught up with the first woman you see, we got to make our rounds." Michael looks back at the table and frowns at Sharon, "Don't worry," he says. Michael continues to look across the room at the other woman but because of the distance he can't place where he knows the woman from.

CHAPTER 11

A WOMAN IN PAIN

Back at Michael's house, nosy Mrs. Crabbs keeps a lookout for him and she also makes sure the police are outside and continues to monitor the events surrounding Michael's residence.

On the other side of Los Angeles a lonely and depressed Ms. Orbison sits in a lonely home contemplating ending her life. This is not the first night that she has considered such drastic measures but tonight the feeling is far stronger than in the past. She shaves the left side of her head and loads a .38 caliber with six bullets, as she is about to pull the trigger the phone rings loudly and she jumps in fear.

"Hello," says a frightened and tearful Ms. Orbison, "who is this?"

"It's Lieutenant Towns," says the voice on the other end," are you ok Ms. Orbison? Ms. Orbison doesn't immediately respond, Ms. Orbison are you there, I just felt the need to call. We're gonna get him but we need you to help us."

"How can I help," asks Ms. Orbison.

"Look out your window," says Lieutenant Towns. "Do you see that car parked in front of your street, that car is there for you."

"I see it," says Ms. Orbison.

"He can't hurt you again," says Lieutenant Towns. "I won't let him, but you gotta stay strong, promise me you'll stay strong, promise me."

Ms. Orbison is quiet for a moment and then whispers back, "I promise." They disconnect their call and Ms. Orbison looks at the gun and puts it back in the drawer where it came from and slowly goes into her bedroom with a slight sense of security knowing the police are watching her 24 hours a day and that in her mind the police are looking for the right person.

CHAPTER 12

CORETTA IS BACK

Back at The Hole in The Wall Michael and Eric are making the rounds and Michael notices that Steve is not there yet.

"I thought you said Steve was gonna meet us here?" asks Michael. "Where is he at?"

"You got me," says Eric, you know he flake sometimes and after seeing all that stuff you went through at Black Long Beach he may not want to be seen with a killer."

"Oh that's funny brother," scoffs Michael, "Dave Chapelle you are not." The time is 9 o'clock and the open Mic session is about to start. The DJ opens up the floor for the club to share their talents and the regulars come up thinking that this is their chance to get a singing contract while others come up and sound so bad that they get the" sandman" treatment and are booed off the floor. Michael continues to order drinks and he is still feeling good from smoking that "spliff" in the car with Eric. He continues to notice several eyes on him but none watch him more intently than the woman across the club that keeps staring at him, she seems to be totally fixated on him.

"Why don't you go say something to her?" asks Eric. "It's rude to stare good brother. Besides, all that shit you talk about being this big time Mack Daddy Gigolo, I know you aren't scared to make a move."

"I'm not scared brother," says Michael. "It's just something about her, I know that woman, but she won't come all the way out in the open so I can see her." As Michael walks away the server approaches with a bottle of Dom Perignon and gives it to Michael.

"I didn't order that," says Michael. "I haven't had Champagne in years."

"You see that woman," says the server pointing to the woman that has been staring at Michael, "her only request is that you join her at her table over there." Michael looks at the Champagne and his mind flashes back to a time five or six years before when a woman sent him the same kind of Champagne with the same request.

"No-o-o," says Michael as the woman finally steps in the open to make herself fully visible, it can't be!!! Michael slowly looks up again and sees his worst nightmare staring him in the face.

"Coretta James," mumbles Michael.

"Who?," asks Gary.

"Coretta James," yells Michael, "of all the people for me to run into. That's the last person I would expect to see."

"Coretta James," says Eric, "isn't she that witch bitch from hell that killed your wife and tried to kill you here and in Jamaica and on and on and on."

"Yes that's her," says Michael. "You're looking at a very beautiful, very ruthless, black female billionaire who will stop at nothing and I mean nothing to get what she wants."

"Oh my God is she fine," says Eric, "and that blue dress is hugging that ass. Long beautiful hair, pretty legs, pretty feet, pretty lips, she is almost flawless. Man I'll go over there and lick her toes right now." Michael just stares at Eric and shakes his head in disgust.

"Man are you serious?" asks Michael, "After all the things I told you that woman did to me you are still drooling over her like that."

"Man, that's one of the finest women I've ever seen in my life. How was the sex?"

"What?" asks Michael.

"You heard me," says Eric. "How was the sex? You told me you got down with her on the first night, how was it? Man I just got a whole new level of respect for you. You bagged that Queen and got millions of dollars out of her."

"Yeah but I almost died several times," says Michael.

"Life's hazards," says Eric callously, "so how good was she."

"I hate to say this," says Michael. "But she was the best I ever had. It was like we were meant to be together, she was soft, feminine and passionate, and". Michael stops in mid sentence "man I can't believe I'm in the middle of the club talking about this, I'm going to send this Champagne back and tell the server to explain to her that I don't want it."

"Explain it to her yourself," says Eric as Michael looks up, "she's standing right behind you." Michael slowly turns around to see the gorgeous Coretta staring him in the face.

CHAPTER 13

MICHAEL THE POET

"Michael Alexander," says Correta. "Mr. Handsome himself. I thought I was a survivor until I saw you. You survived LA, Jamaica and Alabama and everything in between." She tries to kiss Michael but he turns his head.

"Same ole Michael," says Correta. "Still think you're God's gift to women." Michael just stares at Coretta and has a look of amazement at the audacity of Coretta James to not only approach him but to speak to him like nothing has ever happened.

"Where's your big body guard Manu?" asks Michael. "You don't have enough rice anymore to feed his big ass."

"Times change and people change and I needed an upgrade," says Coretta. "I still have people that watch me just not so closely. Manu was a bit too intense."

"I thought you liked intense,"says Michael. Michael and Coretta look into each others eyes with an intense hatred for each other yet with an intense passion.

"You can never get over me Michael," says Correta. "No matter what happens I have a big part of you, a part that you will never know." Eric gazes intently at the interaction between Michael and Coretta and makes an observation.

"I don't know whether to get you guys a room or call in a referee," says Eric, "to say the two of you have unfinished business is the understatement of the year."

"Let's dance Michael," says Coretta as one of the open Mic performers sings a slow song. Michael reluctantly goes to the dance floor and puts his arms around the beautiful Coretta and he doesn't think of all the evil things that she has done but he contemplates the one long night of passion the two shared. As the slow song ends Michael pulls away from Coretta and walks back over to Eric and Coretta returns to her corner of the club.

"I almost thought I was watching a movie," says Eric, "that was intense."

"I hate that Bitch," says Michael. "She is the scum of the earth."

"That's what your mouth says," states Eric, "but your body language tells a whole different story." "Whatever," says Michael. "You seeing things." "Whatever back," says Eric, "I'm sure that deep down you hate her but somewhere inside of you there is a strong pull that you have for that woman, a chemistry that is hard to deny." As Michael and Eric talk, Coretta approaches again.

"My friend Barbara Brown from Florida, remember her, tells me that you are quite the poet," says Coretta to Michael, "recite something for me on the open Mic."

"I don't have any poems that would apply to you," says Michael.

"Write one for me," says Coretta," I'll get you a pen and when you are ready I will tell the DJ to let you recite it, that's if you still have the skills." Michael loves nothing more than a challenge and Coretta retrieves a pen and paper and brings it back to Michael.

"Let's see what your skill set is like," says Coretta. Michael snatches the pen away from Coretta and goes in the corner of the club to one of the sofas and thinks of something that he can put on paper as if he has accepted a challenge to his ego. As Michael sits on the sofa writing and sipping on his drink, Eric just wanders around the club trying to see what he can get into. After about twenty minutes of writing Michael emerges from his little hideaway with a handwritten paper and walks towards Eric.

"I'm about to put her in her place," says Michael.

"You wrote something that fast," says Eric, "you sure you want to go through with this? It's been some serious talent on that Mic tonight and I know you my boy but if it's bad I'll help them boo your ass offstage."

"Thanks for the vote of confidence," says Michael. "With friends like you who needs enemies." Michael looks towards Coretta and motions for her to come over. Coretta approaches with a smile on her face.

"That was fast," says Correta. "How can you write something meaningful that fast."

"You're an easy subject," says Michael. "Tell the DJ I'm ready to go whenever he's ready." Coretta walks over to the DJ and tells him that she wants Michael to recite his work and the DJ acknowledges her.

"Okay Michael," says Correta. "He says that you will be up next as soon as this song has finished. I'm excited to finally get a chance to see your talent." "So am I,'" says Eric sarcastically, I want to be able to walk out with my head up high."

"You don't have anything to worry about," says Michael to Eric, "I'm the one that's going onstage." "Yea but I'm with you and I have a reputation to uphold," says the intoxicated Eric, "they know I'm with you so we'll both look bad." Michael pats Eric on the back and walks towards the Microphone. Michael takes his place in the front waiting for the song to end while Eric sits back like a lost puppy or a man on his way to an execution afraid that the world is about to come to an end. As the song ends the DJ goes to the microphone.

"Ladies and gentleman," says the DJ, "we're gonna change the pace a little bit," says the DJ, "we have a gentleman here by the name of, I'm sorry, what's your name brother?"

"Michael Alexander," says Michael.

"Michael Alexander," repeats the DJ, "Michael is going to recite a poem believe it or not." The DJ looks at the 6ft 5in Michael and makes an observation.

"Big brother like this needs to be playing for the Lakers but he wants to be a poet," says the DJ, "alright let's see what he's got."

Michael steps to the Mic.

"If you don't mind," says Michael. "I would like to call Ms. Coretta James to the middle of the floor," says Michael. "And could you dim the lights?"

"The DJ speaks up," brother acts like he owns the club," says the DJ to several laughs.

"And one more thing," says Michael. "Could you put the spotlight on Coretta please."

"Yeah, put the spotlight on," says the DJ sarcastically.

"Anymore requests brother? This better be a hell of a poem that you're reading." Michael doesn't acknowledge the DJ and starts to read his poem. As he starts to speak a guy from the crowd yells out something.

"Ah this corny bullshit," yells the man.

"Sit your ass down," yells Michael back to the man, "with them tight ass pants on. You better not act like you gonna pick something up motherfucker cause you gonna rip them pants in half." The man acts as if he is going to approach Michael but some security people stop him while some of the people at the club laugh at the man and his tight yellow pants.

"As I was saying before I was rudely interrupted," Michael says staring at his heckler, "I wrote this poem a few moments ago for the beautiful woman standing in the spotlight named Coretta James. I call it, Coretta the Bitch."

"Ouch," says one of the ladies in the crowd intrigued by the title.

"Coretta the bitch," repeats Michael. "The DJ tries to stop Michael as he starts to read.

"Let him read his poem," yells Coretta as the commotion stops, finish your poem Michael," says Coretta intensely.

Coretta the Bitch

There are things about Coretta James I want you to know
She's a billion dollar bitch acting like a two dollar hoe
In an animated series she would play the witch
She would rob from the poor and give it to the rich

The audience looks on in a stunned silence not knowing exactly what to say or feel and Coretta just watches as Michael continues to read.

She let me hit it the very first night
That body of hers is incredibly tight
Pussy so hairy I got down on my knees
I couldn't see the forest for the trees

"Shit," yells one of the customers. The DJ looks at Coretta and the club owners and a couple of the burly bouncers in the club and they are just waiting for the signal to shut Michael up. Until something happens Michael continues to read.

She's a ruthless bitch that killed my wife
And two or three times she almost ended my life
Don't let that killa body cloud your mind

That "cunt" so evil she will rob the blind
She's a no good hoe who is just trying to pass
I bet the Tony the Tiger could get some of that ass
I ran into Tony one night real late
I said how was the pussy Tony, he said it was Grrreat
So the morrow of the poem is don't be me
Things are not always what they appear to be
You think you have an Angel and you're filled with pride
But that Angel is really a ravening wolf inside
And like a roaring lion she will eat you whole
She will devour your body and steal your soul
Coretta will chew you up without a doubt
And after she chews you up she'll spit your ass out
I bought her gifts for Xmas but she said she wanted mo
Even Santa Claus called her a hoe, hoe, hoe

Michael tries to continue to read more but some of the ladies in the club are extremely upset and start yelling at him and the bouncers are close to Coretta and have had enough. Coretta James yells across the floor.

"That was cruel Michael," she says bluntly.

"You asked me to write you a poem," says Michael back. As people yell and scream at Michael two bouncers grab him by the arms.

"Time for you to get your ass out of here," says a bouncer as they carry him towards the entrance. People are still coming as the bouncers throw Michael out the front entrance ripping the right shoulder of his blue suit.

"Get your ass out of here," yells the bouncer, "and don't ever bring your stupid ass back."

"Fuck you, 'yells Michael back. A minute later Eric is escorted to the door as Michael gets up and brushes himself off.

"Why you making me leave?" asks Eric. "I didn't do anything."

"You shouldn't have been with him," says the bouncer.

"You lucky I gotta go home or I would come up there and whup your big ass," Michael says trying to antagonize the bouncer. The huge bouncer looks at the 235 lb Michael.

"Man I'll break a skinny punk like you in half," says the bouncer as he slams the door in Michael's face. Eric just stares at Michael.

"Man I've heard of people having bad days but nothing like this," says Eric, were closer to my house than yours, come on over, I got a bottle of Scotch and some food. Question, why did you write that poem like that, how did you think that was going to go over well."

"I didn't care," says Michael. "That woman has caused me a lot of pain and I wanted her to feel some of it back."

"I think y'all in love with each other, "says Eric.

"What," says Michael. "Man you crazy."

"That's what your mouth say," says Eric, but the way you looked at her and the way she looked at you back, I know what I saw. And even when you were reading that poem she never seemed to lose control."

CHAPTER 14

WRONG PLACE TO BE

As Michael stands up and dusts himself off he notices several women going into a building about a half mile away down long Beach Blvd.

"I wonder where all them fine women going, he says, must be a nice party. Let's go check it out."

"I don't know man," says Eric, as bad as this day is going we don't need any more trouble."

"I can't get any worse," says Michael. "Come on brother I want to hang out with some women before the night ends." Michael walks towards the crowd and Eric reluctantly follows and as they arrive at the building they notice the place is packed.

"Man this seems like a very young crowd," says Eric, man I don't think we need to go in here."

"Man you the scariest brother I know," says Michael. "I'm going in, you just stay here til I get back" Eric doesn't want to be outside by himself and follows Michael into the large building that has no tables and is very crowded. The two men work their way through the crowd and Michael begins to realize that he has dropped in on a gang party. The women have on very short skirts and the men have on jeans with their underwear exposed and bandanas tied around their heads. "Let's get out of here, Michael says, we just walked into the wrong party." As Michael and Eric turn to exit a skinny gang member walks up with a shotgun and hits Michael with the butt end of the gun directly in the stomach.

"Who invited y'all bitch asses to the party," says the man, and why you leaving so soon." Michael gasps for air on the floor as Eric is terrified as several other gang members have surrounded them while the hip hop music stops and everyone stares. Eric is too afraid to talk and Michael is on his knees trying to breathe. The men just stare and Michael stands up in pain and speaks.

"We didn't mean to interrupt your party, he says, we were just passing by and say the crowd. Please let us leave brother."

"I ain't your brother," says the gangster, they call me Bones. That man standing behind you we call him shotgun for obvious reasons and we have hundreds of other brothers standing around you and we don't like people walking into our gatherings, you may be the popo."

"Man we ain't no police," says Michael. "We just in the wrong place at the wrong time. We was down the way at The Hole in The Wall and I read some poetry and got thrown out and we saw the crowd and came over here."

"Poetry," says Shotgun a very dark 5 ft 10 muscular brother, what kind of weak ass shit is that." Michael does not speak he just looks at the gang of brothers staring at him while Eric just looks down in fear.

"Poetry," says Bones. "I'll tell you what, you can earn your way out of here."

"How?" asks Michael.

"Freestyle," says Bones. "Several brothers in here got rap contracts and we love to compete. If I like the way you sound I might let you go. But it can't be no sugar coated bullshit, you better come hard and you better come correct or they gonna find your ass in the dumpster outside." Bones waves his hands and a gangster named Big Frank comes forward.

"You got 3 minutes," says Bones. "Big Frank time his ass. Go."

Michael has never freestyled in his life but he begins to rhyme as if his life depended on it.

" Y'all crawl around and hiss like a snake in the grass, wearing your pants hanging of your ass, thinking that shit makes you look hard, ending peoples life like the hand of God, well here's another thing that I want to say, pants hanging off your ass makes you look real gay, and the real fucked thing that you fake brothers do, all the people you kill seem to look like you, destroying families and the lives of black men, over and over again and again, you real big putting your own kind in a six foot hole, but believe me one day the devil's coming for your soul, and you may feel justified, with pride and a smile a wide, but the things you do are worst than suicide," Michael points at Bones and continues to freestyle.

"He may call you his friend, again and again but soon my brother your life is going to end, and if you knew your history, then it wouldn't be a mystery, and you live by some rules , instead of acting a fool."

"Time," says Big Frank. Bones approaches Michael and just stares in his face. Shotgun points his cannon in Michael's face.

"Let me smoke this Motherfucker Bones," says Shotgun, bitch can't disrespect us like that." Bones lowers the gun and although he hates the words he is impressed with Michael.

"Boy what's your name?" asks Bones. "I ain't never seen a Nigga with balls like you before."

"Michael is my name," he says.

"Michael I'm a man of my word," says Bones. "Since you want to rhyme about God and being gay, when I was little my Grandma told me a Bible story about Sodom and Gomorrah and how the man's wife looked back and turned into a pillow of salt. You and your punk ass boy turn around and head towards the door, don't look left, don't look right, don't look back, walk straight ahead. Disobey me and Shotgun here is going to turn you into a pillow of blood." The crowd parts and the entrance towards the door is revealed. Michael puts his hands in Eric's face towards his eyes to block his peripheral vision and they walk towards the door both trembling with Michael holding Eric's head. The distance is only twenty feet but it seems like two miles. As they reach the door they continue to look straight and cross Long Beach Blvd. and a

Van comes full speed towards them and almost runs them over.

"Man get your stupid ass out the road," yells the driver. Michael and Eric reach the other side of the street and run towards Eric's car still not looking back. As they reach the car Eric is shaking and has a big wet spot in the middle of his pants. He drops his keys on the ground and Michael picks them up.

"Man can you drive?" asks Michael. "You need me to handle it."

"Man fuck you," says Eric, you almost got us killed. I ain't never been that scared in my life." They get into the car and Eric tears out of the parking lot.

CHAPTER 15

FORBIDDEN LOVE AGAIN

As Michael and Eric head towards Eric's Condo in Carson, Sergeant Hall calls Lieutenant Towns with good news.

"Ok," says Sergeant Hall, we will have the search warrant and be over to Mr. Alexander's house by 8am,we will take an entire forensics team and we have an order to get a swab for his DNA. So don't worry it's just a matter of time before we get him."

"No luck with the APB so far," says Lieutenant Towns. "He will turn up and we will be waiting for him when he does. Okay, let's get some sleep so we will be ready in the morning. Goodnight sir."

While the two Detectives make plans for their investigation, Michael and Eric pull up to Eric's Carson, CA condo and notice that they are being followed by a long black Mercedes Benz that is close on their tail. Eric constantly checks his rear view mirror and finally starts to speak to Michael again.

"There's a car that's been following us for a while," says Eric, I'm beginning to think that you are bad luck Sleprock or something." As Eric pulls in front of his Condo the Mercedes Sedan stops directly behind them and the door opens.

"You got your .38 on you?" asks Eric. "We might have trouble more trouble and I don't know how much more I can take."

"Naw man," says Michael. "I left it in my briefcase at that house." The driver of the sedan opens the right rear passenger door and a woman emerges and after a brief conversation the woman asks the driver to leave.

"Are you sure you will be ok?" asks the driver.

"Yes, I will be fine." says the woman. The large driver, a black male about 6'4 inches tall and 300 lbs gives a mean stare at Eric and Michael and drives off. The woman walks to the passenger side of the car and Michael realizes it's Coretta James.

"Can a woman join or is this a boys only party," says Correta. "I don't want to intrude."

"What do you want Coretta?" asks Michael. "You're not gonna shoot me are you."

"If I were going to shoot you you would already be dead," says Correta. "One of my bouncers would have shot you at the club."

"Your bouncers," says Michael. "Don't tell me you own that club too."

"I'm part owner yes," says Correta. "You mind if I come in and hang out with you boys. I've got a $1000 bottle of Whisky and I would hate to drink by myself."

"Only Coretta James would invite herself to someone house and not even be slightly concerned about it," says Michael. "But it's not my house it's up to Eric."

"You got any weapons on you, "asks Eric.

"You want to frisk me and see, "asks Coretta. Coretta is wearing a skin tight blue dress that is too tight to hide anything and the only thing in her hand is the bottle of Scotch. Eric looks at Coretta and thinks there is nothing he would like more than to frisk her but not wanting to seem perverted he just tries to play it off.

"No you good," says Eric, you guys come in and excuse my place." Eric has a nice three bedroom Condo with a modern decor, a patio and a backyard with a fire pit, a table and chairs outside.

"Let's go outside," says Eric, I will light the fire pit and we can indulge in this fine bottle of Scotch out there. Anyway, I want another hit of that blunt I had earlier and maybe it will calm my nerves." Michael and Coretta go outside and Eric grabs some glasses and ice and meets them on the patio. Michael looks at the tear on his new Blue suit.

"I'm going to get you a new suit and tie combo," says Coretta. "Don't worry it will be taken care of tomorrow, how did you get that cut on your shoulder". Michael just stares at Coretta and doesn't say anything. He snatches the bottle of Scotch from her hand and grabs one of the glasses that Eric retrieved and opens the $1000 Scotch and stares at Coretta again.

"Why are you here," says Michael to Coretta.

"Because you are here," says Correta. "No matter what you recited in that club or what you say you think of me, I know you want some of me as bad as I want some of you. I can see it in your eyes, the eyes don't lie. And also, when you hugged me in the club, I felt your little friend down there come to life. I barely touched you. I almost wet my pants, rather my dress." Eric sits there sipping on the Scotch and looking at Michael and Coretta in amazement as they stare at each other as if he isn't there as Michael continues to pretend that he hates Coretta.

"How did you get out of that fire in Jamaica?" asks Michael. "I watched that shit burn down to the ground. I almost shitted my pants when I saw you walk up to me in LA after I sold that Condo, I said this shit can't be real, I thought you were gonna kill me."

"I could never kill you Michael," says Coretta. "At least I couldn't do it myself."

"Well that's comforting,"says Michael. "I guess."

"Let me hit that joint man, Michael says to Eric, this has been the day from hell. You know," says an inebriated Michael, "no more negative talk, we're here together, the three of us, let's just enjoy ourselves." Michael picks up a glass and pours Coretta a shot of her own liquor.

"Thank you sir," says Coretta.

"My pleasure madam," says Michael sarcastically. The three of them sit up drinking and smoking until about 2am and Eric says he is tired. The fire in the outdoor pit feels good and the warm Southern California night makes an inviting evening.

"Do you have a sleeping bag?" asks Coretta. "I want to sleep out here under the fire."

"Yeah I got one but," says Eric, but it's a single meaning that it is only big enough for one person." "Well, I'm only one person," says Correta. "That's all I need." Michael stands up and says he needs to use the bathroom and Eric goes to retrieve the sleeping bag. After Michael comes out of the bathroom, Eric has already passed the sleeping bag onto Coretta and catches Michael coming out.

"You know where the guest room is," says a very" high" and still terrified Eric, I'm going to bed". He staggers into his bedroom and Michael grabs his glass and goes back out into the backyard to pour another drink. He walks into the backyard and he finds Coretta standing in front of the sleeping bag with no clothes on, waiting for him,

"I knew you was coming back out here," says Correta. "I have a sleeping bag waiting for you, I know you're tired, let's go to sleep."

Michael doesn't even try to play as if he doesn't want to be with Coretta, he just enjoys the site of the beautiful Coretta and he pours himself another drink.

"Take off your clothes Michael," says Correta. "Let's enjoy the fire. The last time we were rushed into what we did, this time let's just enjoy the night." Michael takes off his clothes and the two of them enjoy the fire as Eric pretends to be asleep. Michael and Coretta enjoy the expensive alcohol and talk to each other with no clothes on as a drunk Eric looks on through the window like a peeping Tom. As the time moves on the California night starts to get cold with the breeze coming from the ocean. Coretta wants to get inside the sleeping bag and she wants Michael to get inside the sleeping bag with her. He is very drunk and easily agrees to get inside the sleeping bag with Coretta. The bag is only big enough for one but it is a perfect fit for two people that want to be close to each other. Coretta gets into the bag and Michael joins her inside the bag and the two zip each other together and their bodies become one. Before the bag is zipped up Michael and Coretta begin to make passionate love to each other with no room between the two of them. Although Michael claims that he hates Coretta he penetrates her and makes love to her like a long lost love that he is glad to have come in contact with again. The connection between them is incredible as they take advantage of each others bodies like they have never been with another person before. They enjoy the time with each other for as long as they can and after making sure that they each is satisfied, they fall asleep in each others arms in the tight sleeping bag huddled so close together that there is no room for one to move without the other moving also. It was a truly special night for the both of them and they both snore the night away.

CHAPTER 16

MICHAEL FACES THE MUSIC

At about 10am the next morning Eric comes to the kitchen and looks out the window and sees Michael alone in the sleeping bag. Eric walks outside and Michael is fast asleep inside the sleeping bag seemingly without a care in the world. Eric walks to the front and finds his front door closed but unlocked. He walks to the backyard and wakes up Michael from his deep sleep.

"Wake up sleeping beauty," says Eric to Michael, you gonna sleep the day away." Michael is really groggy and can barely comprehend what Eric is saying.

"Get your ass up boy," says Eric to Michael, you are sleeping like you work nights. That fine ass Coretta left you out here in the yard by yourself." Eric checks the fire in the pit and everything is out and he checks out the area. He notices Michael's underwear thrown around the yard and realizes that Michael is naked inside the sleeping bag. Michael starts to stand up from the sleeping bag.

"Hold up brother," says Eric, I don't want to see your naked ass get out of that sleeping bag. Just keep that bag over you and get your clothes." Michael gets up and carries the sleeping bag over him and looks inside the bag and realizes what went on between himself and Coretta. Eric is still feeling the effects of the night himself but has some insight for Michael.

"So you call this woman all kinds of bitches in front of a crowd of people, call her a hoe, a slut and every name known to man, yet she comes over here and fucks your eyeballs out," says Eric, I have never saw anything like it before. They can't make this shit up, I'm gonna call Oprah and see if she can put this shit on OWN."

"Don't call her fat ass,"says Michael. "I don't have enough chicken wings to pay her for the story."

"You better cut that shit out," says Eric, she will have Gayle come over her and whup your ass with those big hoot owl glasses on. Or she will wake up Steadman and then you really got problems."`

"I'll fuck Steadman and Gayle up," says Michael. "And anybody else she got. I got us away from them gang brothers didn't I."

"Get your drunk ass up and don't mention that shit to me again," says Eric, let me take you to get your car so you can take your ass home and get some rest, you need it."

"You need it to Nigga," says Michael. "You the one had me smoking that bullshit last night."

"I didn't push that shit down your throat," says Eric, you hit it for yourself. It's just like riding a horse, all you gotta do is get back in the saddle."

"Fuck you," says Michael. "Where are my clothes." Michael and Eric look around and his clothes are missing including some of his underwear.

"Where my shit at man?" asks Michael. "All my clothes are gone."

"I don't know," says Eric, you better ask your bitch."

"I don't have a female dog," says Michael. "You better watch your mouth ."

"You didn't have any problem calling her a bitch last night," says Eric, what's the problem now." Michael has no clothes or keys or means to get home.

"Give me something to put on," says Michael. "I need something to wear home." Eric is a little over six foot tall and thicker than Michael so anything Eric has won't fit Michael so he grabs a blue track suit and gives it to Michael and gives him and old pair of white size 11 sneakers, Michael wears a size 14 shoe. Michael squeezes on the tight sweat suit which only reaches his ankles and wears the shoes with the back of his heels sticking out.

"Man I look crazy," says Michael. "Come on man take me to the dealership to get my car."

"Nobody gonna see you," says Eric, I'll take you home first so you can change your clothes."

"Let me use your phone," says Michael. "I need to call the dealership."

"Ok," says Eric. "She took your shoes too."

"She took everything," says Michael. "She even took my draws, I guess she took them."

"I hope she took them," says Eric knowing where Michael's underwear is, I don't want to see your dirty draws in my backyard."

As the two men drive towards Michael's house little do they know that there is a large reception party waiting for them, forensic people, investigators and Sergeant Hall and Lieutenant Towns leading the charge. They have been waiting there since 8:30 that morning for Michael to arrive and they wonder if he has been somehow tipped off to their presence.

"You think he knows we're here waiting for him, asks Lieutenant Towns ,maybe he is on the run."

"I guess it's possible," says Sergeant Hall," one of his neighbors could have called him and told him what was going on."

"How can he run without a car," says Lieutenant Towns. "The dealership dropped it off this morning." "That's one of the reasons I believe he's coming home," says Sergeant Hall," something tells he doesn't even know we're here, I wish we could just break the door down and go in." As the officers continue to talk Mrs. Crabbs continues to monitor both sides of the street looking at the police presence and waiting for Michael. About ten minutes away from the condo Michael and Eric slowly make their way to Michael's home.

"Well I talked to the dealership and they already dropped my car off this morning and left it out front," says Michael. "Even though I told them I would pick it up myself. They say they tried to call me which is very possible because I was probably sleep and my cell phone is in my pants."

"Why would she steal your clothes?" asks Eric. "She must be seriously obsessed with you."

"Look man," says Michael. "Turn down Burbank Drive and it will take us through the backstreet of my house and that way I can come in through my backyard. I leave that window cracked for just such an emergency."

"What about the alarm, asks Eric. "It will go off but it's right by the kitchen," says Michael. "I will turn it right off as soon as I get in." Soon Eric and Michael pull up to the back of his house and as soon as Michael opens the window the alarm goes off alerting the police and a nosy Mrs. Crabb has spotted two men in Michael's backyard. Michael makes it in through the window and turns off the alarm as Mrs. Crabbs tells the police there are two burglars in Michael's backyard. The police quickly race to the backyard.

"Get on the ground, Sherman Oaks police, get on the ground, yells the police at Eric as Michael hears the commotion, put your hands behind your head." Eric hits the ground in terror and does exactly what the police say as Michael opens the back door and yells at the police.

"Man what the hell y'all doing in my yard, yells Michael, why y'all got my boy on the ground like that." The police order Michael to put his hands up and handcuff him also as the rest of the police run around the back closely followed by Mrs. Crabbs.

"Man y'all better get the fuck off me, yells Michael to the police while Eric is set up straight, I'm gonna sue y'all ass for this."

"That's him, yells Mrs. Crabbs, that's Michael Alexander right there."

"Mr. Alexander, I am Sergeant Dewayne Hall and this is Lieutenant Towns of the Sherman Oaks police department, why were you breaking into your own home. Did you realize there was a police presence in front. Who tipped you off"?

"I told you he was no good," says Mrs. Crabbs," he always got people in and out, especially different women, all hours of the night."

"Shut your old ugly ass up Mrs. Crabbs, shouts Michael, what I do in my house is my business. Why don't you take your old ass home and trim your toenails or play with ugly ass rat dogs you got over there."

"How dare you talk about my babies like that," says Mrs. Crabbs. As Mrs. Crabbs is talking Sergeant Hall cuts her off.

"Will someone escort this woman back to her home please, he says, we'll take it from here ma'am." Mrs. Crabbs is still mumbling under her breath as she walks off.

"Yeah take her old ass home," says Michael. "And take them handcuffs off my boy. Now," says Michael. "What is this shit all about."

"We have court order to search your property Mr. Alexander," says Lieutenant Towns ,we are investigating a rape and sodomy act that was reported to us by Ms. Darlene Orbison."

"Darlene Orbison," says Michael. "That's the woman I showed the house to yesterday, she ran out screaming as if she had seen a ghost."

"Or a rapist," says Lieutenant Towns.

"You better watch your mouth lady," says Michael. "I have never forced myself on a woman in my life." Michael is still handcuffed and Lieutenant Towns approaches him.

"My name is Lieutenant Towns, she says, not lady and you will address me accordingly." Michael turns up his nose at the officer.

"What's your first name lady, he says , your momma didn't name you Lieutenant did she?" Sergeant Hall steps in between the two as the Lieutenant wants to hurt Michael.

"Can I get these cuffs off please," says Michael. "I can't rob my own house." Sergeant Hall directs the officer to take off the handcuffs and he immediately slaps the court order into his hands.

"Mr. Alexander," says Sergeant Hall, would you mind opening the front door so our forensic team can come in."

Michael looks at the court order and realizes that he has no choice but to abide by it. As he moves back into his house to open the front door he notices Lieutenant Towns frowning at him intensely.

"You need to get you some," says Michael to Lieutenant Towns, that's your problem.

" Never from you," mumbles the Lieutcnant.

"You got that right," says Michael. "You couldn't handle this, you probably like women anyway." "Mr. Alexander," says Sergeant Hall," would you open the front door please." Michael slowly moves forward and opens the front door for the Forensic people to come in. As the Forensic people surrounded by police enter into Michael's home, one woman stops and tells Michael

"Mr. Alexander we have a court order to get a copy of your DNA," says the woman, we will need a swab of your cheeks and a strand of your hair. Open your mouth wide please sir."

"Get the fuck away from me," says Michael. "I ain't giving you shit. Swab my cheeks for what"?

"Swab your cheeks so we can see if you are the pervert we believe you are," says Lieutenant Towns. "Open your mouth before I have one of the officers hold it open for you, the way you made Ms. Orbison hold open her legs while you stuck that bottle up her crotch."

"Fuck you bitch," says Michael. "Touch me and you'll pull back a nub." Lieutenant Towns advances towards Michael but Sergeant Hall stops her and shakes his head.

"Mr. Alexander we have a court order to get your DNA," says Sergeant Hall, if you are an innocent man as you claim to be then you have nothing to worry about." Eric stands back in the cut watching the whole situation in amazement. As Michael spars with the police a black Mercedes limo pulls up in front of his house. He looks out front and realizes that the limousine belongs to Coretta and walks towards the car watched closely by the police. Coretta rolls down the window in the back as she sees all the police presence.

"What the hell Michael, she says, what's up with all these dirty ass blue bloods out here."

"Coretta," says Michael. "Where the hell are my clothes."

"I wanted to replace your suit," says Correta. "You were sleeping so hard I thought I would be able to get you a new suit and be back before you got up."

"Yea," says Michael. "You left me buck ass necket in the backyard, and why did you take my draws?"

"I didn't take your draws," says Correta. "You left them somewhere in that yard, don't worry they're gonna turn up." As the two of them talk the police listen intently hoping to hear something incriminating.

"Call a lawyer Michael, she says as she gives him his old suit and the new suit she purchased for him, if you need someone I got somebody. I took your phone out and put my new number in it, you better put a code on that phone so no one can get your info." She rolls up her window and has her driver take off, she has a copy of Michael's contact info, text info and all his information from his phone, just for future references. Michael realizes that he needs some help to handle the situation that he is in. Instead of trying to wait to call a contact of Coretta's, he calls someone he knows will have his back, he calls Cheryl Bolling, Kenneth's wife.

CHAPTER 17

LEGAL WOES

Cheryl is out shopping and answers Michael's call on the second ring.

"This is Attorney Bolling, answers Cheryl, how can I help you today."

"Cheryl, he says, this is Michael, how are you?"

"Long time no talk to," says Cheryl. "How are you Mr. Alexander, to what do I owe the privilege of this call."

"How are you my friend," says Michael, 'I'm glad that you have the same phone number, I need some legal advice."

"So this is not a social call, she asks, what have you got yourself into now?"

"I'm sorry that I haven't called," says Michael. "After all the stuff we went through with Ken I just wanted to let you do your thang. I figured you and Gary were making things happen."

"Gary and I didn't work out," says Cheryl. "It was good for a minute but we decided to go our separate ways, you know how it goes."

"I'm sorry," says Michael.

"Don't be," says Cheryl. "That's how life goes, he was loyal to Barbara Brown and very devoted to her, so what's going on Michael."

"I'm not sure, he says, the police are over here turning my house upside down."

"What are they looking for Michael, she asks, what did they say you did?"

"They say I raped some woman, he states, they have a warrant and they are asking for a swab of my cheeks and a strand of my hair."

"Why do they believe you did it, asks Cheryl, what do they say they have?"

"I was showing a house yesterday," says Michael. "And apparently the woman that I was showing the house to, a Ms. Orbison, was raped six or seven months ago and somehow she confuses me for the man that raped her."

"How's that possible, replies Cheryl, why would she think it was you, is she one of your former conquests."

"Of course not," says Michael. "And for the record I have never forced myself on a woman in my life and I never will."

"Yeah I know Michael," says Cheryl. "I've known you for years and I have never known you to be that way. Okay, they are going to want to take you to the police station to interrogate you."

"So what do I tell them"? he asks.

"Nothing," says Cheryl. "Cooperate, go with them to the station and I will meet you there. We don't want it to appear that you have anything to hide." "Okay, he says, I'm on my way back inside now and I will meet you at the precinct."

"Mr. Alexander," says Sergeant Hall," we need you to come down to the station and give us a statement."

"I was just going to change my clothes," says Michael. He goes upstairs to change his clothes as Lieutenant Towns calls Ms. Orbison who answers immediately.

"Ms. Orbison," says the Lieutenant, I'd like for you to come back down to the police station, we will be interviewing Mr. Alexander and I would like for you to take another look at him and verify that he is the one that assaulted you."

"What if he sees me," says Ms. Orbison, I don't want him to see me."

"He won't," says the Lieutenant, it's a one way mirror, you can see him but he can't see you, don't worry you will be perfectly safe." Ms. Orbison reluctantly agrees to come down to the station and as soon as Michael is dressed he accompanies the two police down to the station to answer questions. As he starts to leave his home a forensics person asks for a swab of his cheeks and a strand of hair.

"No way," says Michael to the Tech, I will wait till I see my Attorney".

"We have a court order," says Lieutenant Towns rudely, you have no choice." Sergeant Hall stops Lieutenant Towns and uses reverse psychology.

"I thought you said you didn't do it," says Sergeant Hall, an innocent man should not have a problem giving his DNA." Michael just stares at the Sergeant and looks him in the face.

"I can't believe you trying to run that lame ass game on me," says Michael. "And for the record I am 100 percent innocent. Take your damn swab and I just had my hair cut a couple of days ago so watch the doo." After getting the samples they finally head towards the police station to interview him as his Attorney and friend Cheryl Bolling arrives at the police station. As Cheryl arrives at the police station she overhears two policemen talking.

"Yeah I think they are going to bring in that rape suspect Michael Alexander for interrogation," says the officer, and what Mr. Alexander doesn't know is that they have surveillance from not only the rape of Darlene Orbison but also several other LA area rapes and we clearly have Mr. Alexander on video leaving the scene of several crimes. We have DNA and fingerprints and if all matches up we have enough to put him away for life. He is walking into the station soon but he is not going to walk out."

CHAPTER 18

FUGITIVES

After hearing the policeman talk she walks outside and hopes that the Detectives pull up in front of the building with Michael. Shortly afterwards a police car pulls up with Michael. Atty. Bolling immediately rushes to the car before they take their prisoner inside.

"I'm Attorney Cheryl Bolling and I would like a few moments to speak with my client before we go inside," says Cheryl as the Sergeant and Lieutenant stand and watch, can I have a moment of privacy, I will bring him right in." The two Detectives reluctantly walk inside as Michael and Cheryl watch their movements and as soon as the door closes Cheryl starts to run towards her car and encourages Michael to also run.

"Come on Michael, she says, you gotta get out of here, if you go inside they are going to arrest you."

"What do you mean," says Michael.

" I'll explain in the car," says Cheryl. "Just haul your ass." The two of them jump in Cheryl's car and spin out of the parking lot as Ms. Orbison pulls up and sees Michael speeding out of the parking lot with an unknown woman driving. As Sergeant Hall and Lieutenant Towns enter the building one of their fellow officers starts relaying information about Michaels case.

"Sergeant Hall," says the officer, we got your man Mr. Alexander dead to right, we have footage of him coming in and out of the building at the scene of Ms. Orbison's assault and we also have footage from the buildings of several other sex crimes with him also leaving the buildings, including that woman in Pasadena who was raped and murdered, it's as if he was posing for the camera, he wasn't even trying to hide. By the way, where is Mr. Alexander." As the officer speaks a very afraid Ms. Orbison walks into the precinct and stares down Lieutenant Towns.

"I thought you said you would have him under control," says Ms. Orbison, I just saw him speeding out of the driveway with some woman." The officers rush towards the door but the car is already gone. They run back inside the precinct,

"Let's get a BOLO out for Michael Alexander and his Attorney," says Sergeant Hall, I think her name was Cheryl Bolling."

"How could you let them get away like that," says an officer," looks like they played you."

"We had no choice but to leave them," says Sergeant Hall, we have to respect the Attorney client privilege. I wonder what made her run, maybe she overheard something, were you guys in here talking about the case."

They look at each other but no one speaks.

"Well whatever the case, let's find them and in the meantime we will wait for the swab from his cheeks to come back and let's look at some of that video footage," says Sergeant Hall, don't worry we'll catch him.

`Back in the car,

"Cheryl," says Michael," what was that all about, you're the one that told me to cooperate and now we're running. And why are we running"? Cheryl checks the rear view mirror to make sure they are not being followed as she talks to Michael.

"They were about to lock you up, she says , they say they have video evidence of you leaving the scene of some of the rapes and one rape turned into a murder, I've known you for years and I know it would be very hard for you to do a night in jail let alone the rest of your life."

"The rest of my life," says Michael.

"Michael, she says, felony rape and sodomy along with probably a charge of kidnapping and murder carries a life sentence and California still has the death penalty even though they haven't used it in years and they may not give you a bail, they may consider you a flight risk because of all your connections."

"But you believe me when I say I'm innocent don't you Cheryl?" asks Michael. "I would never do that." "Michael I've known you for years and I have never known you to be forceful with a woman," says Cheryl. "And when they started talking about anal stuff I knew that definitely wasn't you. You always talk about not wanting anything in the ass area."

"But Cheryl what will we do, he asks, and you just destroyed your life over me. Now where will we go?"

"There's a cheap motel on Adams Ave downtown on skid row," says Cheryl. "Real cheap and cash only, once we get there go to your bank and withdraw all the cash you can and we have to lay low until we find a way to prove that you didn't do this shit"

"You straight gangster," says Michael. "I didn't know you had it in ya."

"I live in the burbs Michael but I was born in the hood," says Cheryl. "They will never look for us down here and we can kind of hide in plain sight." The two of them pull up to the trashy motel which reminds Michael of home because he once lived down there.

"I don't have my piece," says Michael. "We need something down here." Cheryl reaches into her purse and pulls out a semi automatic .380 handgun and Michael just looks at her.

"All these years and I never really knew you, he says, let's get to it." Cheryl goes to retrieve the room while Michael remains in the car.

"How many nights can I get the room for," asks Cheryl.

"As many nights as you want, are you going to bring your Johns through here also," asks the attendant.

"I'm not a hooker," says Cheryl. "Can I park my car around the back?" She has a red convertible V12 Mercedes Benz with a monogrammed license plate.

"You might want to park that nice car up front," says the attendant, there are some rough "cats" around here and that car might not be safe. And the rooms are $39.99 a night."

"Here's $120 dollars for 3 nights," says Cheryl.

"That's $164.00," says the attendant,8 percent sales tax. She gives the man the money and walks off and he notices how beautiful she is and how incredible her body is.

"If you get lonely on one of the late nights please let me know," says Sam the attendant, my name is Sam and my friends all came me Sam I am." "Don't hold your breath Sam I am," says Cheryl. "That's an invitation you will never get. You'd be much better off with green eggs and ham."

Cheryl gets in the car and drives around the backside as the room is also in the back on the first floor and she tries to park her car directly in front of her room where she can see it through the window and the two of them walk into room 109.The room looks like a $40 room in downtown LA, one twin size bed with dingy sheets and one small cover ,a 32 inch TV, a green carpet with holes in it, one chair in the room, a bathroom with a few very thin towels that don't look very clean to begin with and neither does the bathroom, and of course a toilet. Cheryl calls her favorite cousin Elliot and asks for a favor.

"Cuzo, she says, I need a favor and please don't ask me to explain."

"Ok," says Elliot, what do you need, baby girl"?

"I need you to let me park my car in your garage for a few days," she says," I'll come and pick it up when I need it." Elliot was once married but now lives alone and has a two car garage but only one car.

"What's wrong Cuz?" he asks. "Are you going out of town?"

"I'll explain later," she replies, "and I also need you to rent me a car, I need to be incognito for a while." Elliot loves his cousin Cheryl unconditionally and tells Cheryl he will do whatever she needs him to do.

"Thanks Elliot, she says, I will get the car to you within the hour and I need you to rent that car for me today and put it in your name." Cheryl hangs up the phone and immediately calls AAA and tells them to pick up the car at the hotel and gives them her cousins address to have the car delivered. Although the skid row area is slightly off the grid there are decent places to go and Cheryl instructs Michael.

"Michael , who do you bank with?" Michael gives Cheryl the name of his bank and after looking for a location they find one within a six block radius and she instructs him to get as much cash as he possibly can and she will do the same just in case something comes up. Michael is amazed at her.

"What did you do read gangster 101,he asks, I'm wondering if I ever knew you at all."

"I'm from the hood Michael remember," says Cheryl. "You can take the girl out of the hood but you can't take the hood out of the girl. And besides I'm also a lawyer so I have lived on both sides of the track and I've seen it all. You go to your bank and I will wait for AAA and I'm going to wait for my cousin to bring me the car and while I'm at his house I'm going to get us some sheets and towels and cleaning stuff, no way I'm touching any of this stuff." Michael is not only amazed that Cheryl has 100 percent faith in his innocence but that she is willing to put her life on the line for his wellbeing.

CHAPTER 19

THE EVIDENCE

While the two of them try to put things together downtown, the SOPD have received copies from the DNA sample that Michael gave.

"Sergeant," says one the police officers, "we have a match not only is Mr. Alexander guilty of raping and sodomizing Darlene Orbison but his DNA matches several other rapes over the last 18 months including the rape and murder of Donna Stone."

"Wow," says the Sergeant, that sick Motherfucker. I wonder if that lawyer knew all that before she ran off with him."

"I looked her up too," says an officer, "Cheryl Bolling formerly Cheryl Johnson was married to Ken Bolling, who, get this, molested children."

"Wow," says Lieutenant Towns," she really can pick them."

"And get this," says the officer, "Ken Bolling was killed by none other than Michael Alexander's uncle as Mr Bolling was allegedly trying to molest Mr. Alexander's daughter Brittany. Mrs. Bolling has a sterling reputation not only in the community but also amongst her peers, not even a traffic ticket, said to be of impeccable character. Turns out she has known Mr. Alexander for many years, was his wife's best friend and is godmother to his daughter.

"Wow," says Sergeant Hall, even with all that I can't believe she would risk it all for a rapist. We need to find her also because if she doesn't know about the DNA, she could end up being the next victim. Put out a BOLO for Cheryl Bolling also." As Sergeant Hall is about to leave a Detective calls him over.

"Sarge," says the Detective, you're gonna want to see this." Sergeant Hall goes over to the video screen and at each crime scene that Michael is accused of being part of there is video evidence of Michael actually entering and leaving the crime scenes.

"Look at this bold Motherfucker," says Lieutenant Towns. "He's not even trying to hide, it's as if he is looking for the camera."

"I have never seen anyone this bold before," says Sergeant Hall, sick fucker. We gotta get him off the streets, call the CBI(California Bureau of Investigation)and call the news stations and let's get the footage out so the public can see it and, call the newspapers, we need all hands on deck."

As the police Officers scramble to get Michael off the streets the two fugitives have both retrieved money from their banks and sit in the room as Cheryl's cousin pulls up to the room in the rental.

"Okay Michael, she says, that's my cousin outside, don't leave the room or do anything until I get back."

"Where is your car," says Michael. "Someone stole it that fast."

"No, she says, AAA got it while you were at the bank, my cousin put it in his garage because I'm sure they are looking for me as well by now, don't worry we will figure this thing out, until then stay put." Cheryl gets in the car with her cousin Elliot and heads to drop him off at his home.

"Cousin what you doing down here in this piece of shit Motel," says Elliot, I can't let you come back down here to this. Do you know the kind of riff raff that hangs out in this part of town."

"I'll be fine," says Cheryl. "I just need a getaway for a few days. No matter who asks ,you haven't seen me or heard from me, okay ".

"What about Aunt Lisa," asks Elliot.

"Especially her, she states, my mother definitely doesn't need to know where I am, it would worry her to death."

"Promise me cousin," says Cheryl. "Promise me."

"Ok," says Elliot reluctantly, I promise."

CHAPTER 20

THE RETURN OF A FRIEND

As Elliot drives the 2005 Chevrolet Impala rental towards his home Michael suddenly remembers a friend that lives in the skid row area and calls to see if his number remains the same.

"Hello," says the voice on the other line.

"I'm looking for Donald Cook," says Michael.

"This is Donald Cook," says the voice on the other line, who this."

"Dr. Cook, yells Michael, man you're still hanging in there."

"Is this who I think it is," says Donald, only one person calls me Dr. Cook, Michael Alexander, is that you my man."

"In the flesh brother," says Michael. "I can't believe you got the same number, I'm at the Kensington on Adams Avenue."

"What you doing in that piece of shit?" asks Donald. "Even I wouldn't stay there."

"It's a long story," says Michael. "Are you still down here, I also heard you had been sick"

"In Rehab but I'm better now," says Donald, off the crack but I still drink, man I'm about six blocks from you on Wilshire, there's a dive bar called The Manhattan about three blocks from where you are, can you make it there, man I haven't seen you in years." Michael remembers Cheryl telling him to stay put but of course he wouldn't miss a chance to see Donald Cook. It's about 7 in the evening and it is starting to get dark outside.

"How long will it take you to get there?" asks Michael.

"Twenty minutes," says Donald Cook. "I'm already dressed and I have already did the 3 S's, shit, showered and shaved, so I'm good."

"See you in twenty brother," says Michael. As Michael prepares to go to the Manhattan to meet Donald police all around the Southern California area search for Michael and Cheryl and her car. Police have posted up outside of Michael house and Cheryl's house and believe that there is no way she can stay out of sight with her red convertible so they feel like it is only a matter of time before they are found. The police check for pings on various cell towers but find no hits believing that the fugitives have discarded their cell phones. The police have released copies of the videos from the various attacks to local and national media and have contacted local and national newspapers to make sure that the story is ran in the morning edition of the papers, a full blitz media campaign has just begun and soon Michael will be the most vilified man in America. Michael walks 4 blocks up from the drug infested

Kensington motel on Adams to a small mostly white dive bar called the Manhattan and goes in looking for Donald and finds him close to the entrance waiting for him to arrive. A Big muscular 6ft 9 inch 320 lb Black bouncer pats Michael down and allows him to enter the club.

"Donald Cook, "says Michael as he embraces Donald. You looking good boy." Donald is about 5 ft 6 inches tall and no longer has the big stomach that was his trademark although he now walks with a slight limp.

"What happened?" asks Michael. "You got a little hitch in your giddy up there."

"I was in a bad car accident," says Donald, messed my leg up pretty bad, it took me two years to learn to walk again. I use this cane now to get around but I'm getting there, I got a couple hundred thousand dollars out of the deal but money can't buy me a new leg."

"Well you still look good man," says Michael. "Let's have a drink."

"Ok," says Donald. "You look the same man except you cut off those curly locks. You still Gigoloing?"

"Naw man," says Michael. "I left that shit alone." Michael and Donald approach the bar of the Manhattan, a dark club/bar with two pool tables in front, tables spread out in the middle of the floor with a DJ next to the floor playing old school white and black pop music. The owner recognizes Donald as being somewhat of a regular and Donald introduces Michael.

"Donald," says the owner, "good to see you back again, who you got with you."

"Mr. Johns," says Donald. "Good to see you too, this my friend Michael Alexander, a good friend from way back that called me out of the blue, so we came out to have one."

"Nice to meet you Michael," says Mr. Johns," your first drink is on me, what will you have." Michael looks at the bar and doesn't see his usual drink so he orders a Johnnie Walker Black and Donald says he will have the same. The white female bartenders are attractive with short shorts on and some of the guests of the club are dressed in the same manner. The music is loud and the smoke in the club is thick like a fog and Michael looks around and spots some decent sites.

"Some of these white girls are fine in here, he says , I'm much more partial to sisters though." "Yea I remember," says Donald, but I know you dibble and dabble every now and then."

"No comment, answers Michael, what happens in Vegas stays in Vegas."

"Got ya,"says Donald, but this ain't Vegas."

As Michael and Donald talk the bartender gives them their drinks and they thank Mr. Johns and walk around.

"You get down here a lot Donald?" asks Michael. "People seem to know you on a first name basis." "Not really," says Donald," since the accident I can't get around like I used to, I can come here because it is close to home."

"Why do you still live down here?" asks Michael. "You like the slums?"

"I got a nice spot up the street," says Donald, they have built it up really nice around here now, it's still slummy in some spots, like that shit hole Kensington you called me from, but it's a lot better than it used to be. Why you staying over there anyways?"

"Long story," says Michael. "Long story." As the two men talk the huge bouncer comes and acknowledges Michael and speaks and flexes his muscles so the men can see them.

"What brings you boys out tonight?" asks the bouncer. "You guys looking for some pink toes.

"Not really brother," says Michael. "Just hanging out for a minute."

"Yeah," says the bouncer ,a lot of brothers come down here to get at the white girls, its all good as long as they don't try to mess with my girl over there at the bar." The bouncer is letting Michael know that his girl is off limits.

"My girl is so fine that I always have to keep my eye on her, "says the bouncer. Michael looks over towards the bar expecting to see a beautiful woman.

"Which one is your girl brother?" asks Michael. "Wouldn't want to make that mistake."

"That's her in the middle of the bar with the white shorts on." Michael looks towards the bar and see a heavy set white woman, very unattractive with white shorts on and what looks like a front tooth missing eating on what appears to be a steak sandwich. Michael points at the woman.

"That's her right there, "he asks in astonishment.

"It's rude to point," says the huge bouncer.

"Sorry," says Michael. "Is that her?"

"Yea," says the bouncer, that's my baby." Michael takes another look to make sure he didn't make a mistake and begins to frown.

"Don't sweat it my friend, he says, you ain't got nothing to worry about."

"What," yells the bouncer. Michael backtracks.

"What I mean, he says, no man in his right mind would dare challenge a man of your stature." The bouncer gives Michael a mean look and walks off.

"Why didn't you just tell that big fucker his woman is ugly?" asks Donald. "Real ugly."

Michael looks back at the gigantic black man. "Okay then," he says, "you go tell him."

"Hell no," replies Donald.

CHAPTER 21

WALLS ARE CLOSING IN

As the two men continue to talk over the loud music Michael notices that the large screen TV over the bar playing the Laker game has been interrupted for a special news bulletin. The news flash says "have you seen this man" and immediately below the caption Michael sees his face and his name and the words "wanted for rape and murder, probably armed and extremely dangerous,$50000 reward and numbers to call if he is spotted. The bulletin says that he was last seen with his Attorney Cheryl Bolling in a red convertible Mercedes Benz headed eastbound on the 10 freeway. Michael immediately turns around and holds his head down and talks to Donald and since Donald was not looking at the television he doesn't know why Michael is so spooked.

"What's wrong with you man?" asks Donald. "You look like you saw a ghost."

"I did," says Michael," Look, I'm in room 109 at the Kensington, I gotta go." Michael runs past the big bouncer and heads straight for the hotel approximately four blocks away. He notices police cars in the area which is not unusual for that part of town. Michael spots a liquor store and takes the chance to go in and buy alcohol with everything that is going on. He walks into the store and grabs a bottle of scotch and heads for the counter holding his head down as he puts the scotch on the counter.

"That will be $75.99 with tax," says the oriental male store keeper. Michael hands him the money and looks away as the store TV also has on the news and he sees his face plastered all over the place. He gives the man a $100 bill and rushes out of the store without asking for his change. Switchboards all over the city are being alerted to possible sightings of Michael including a call from the Manhattan club and a call from the liquor store owner but the police only deal with the calls that they believe are the most credible. Michael races back to the 'seedy motel and realizes he has no keys and he knocks on the door where fortunately Cheryl has made it back to the room. Cheryl has been watching some of the news and wonders what she has gotten herself into. The surveillance tapes of Michael leaving the scene of several crime scenes, and the news of his DNA match leave Cheryl shaken. As she watches the news she jumps in fear as Michael knocks on the door. As he knocks on the door Cheryl doesn't know what to do and is frozen in fear.

"Cheryl open the door, yells Michael, what are you doing." He realizes that Cheryl is probably watching the news like everybody else and pleads for her to open the door.

"Please Cheryl, pleads Michael, I didn't do it, please Cheryl give me a chance, you know me better than this." The sound of his banging on the door causes others to look outside their motel window and Michael doesn't want to be spotted.

"Cheryl please, he cries, don't leave me out here like this, please Cheryl."

"Hey man take your ass home, yells a man in another motel room, can't you see she don't want you."

"Shut your ass up," says Michael. "And mind your own business." Cheryl reluctantly peeps out the door and looks at a desperate Michael and slowly opens the door and he rushes in. Michael motions towards Cheryl who jumps back.

"Cheryl, he says, you gotta believe me, I didn't do this. I can't explain what's going on but I didn't rape or kill anybody."

"But Michael, she says, they got your DNA and they got you on camera leaving the scene. That DNA is impossible to explain, there's a 99.9 chance that it is correct and the chance of it being someone other than you is approximately one in a billion or more."

"Look Cheryl," says Michael as he slowly takes her hand, I can't explain it right now but I would never do these things and you know that." Cheryl sees the sincerity in Michael's eyes and although she doesn't completely believe him she no longer fears him and asks questions.

"But how is it possible, she says, there is no way to explain the DNA."

"Maybe someone stole a sample from me somehow," says Michael. "Is that possible?"

"Not in this case, she says, they got the DNA from bite marks and your sperm, I mean from sperm left inside of the victims. Michael there is no way to explain away the evidence." Cheryl looks in his hands and sees the bottle of Scotch.

"I thought I told you to stay in the room anyway," says Cheryl. "Where did you go."

"To a little dive bar called The Manhattan, he answers, I just needed to get out for a little while." With all the excitement going on Michael forgets to tell Cheryl about his meeting with Donald.

"Well what are you waiting for, asks Cheryl, open up that scotch, I haven't had a drink in a while so I might as well get drunk, my life appears to be over." Michael opens the scotch and he and Cheryl drink and watch the news footage and try to drown their sorrows.

CHAPTER 22

THE SEARCH IS ON

Back at police headquarters the SOPD gets a call and patches it in to Lieutenant Towns.

"Lieutenant Towns," says the dispatch, this is Officer Frank Davis of the LAPD and we've got a homicide down here that matches the MO of your rapist, I'm sending the DNA sample out and we should get a hit by morning. I've been following the news and when we got here and saw the victim Mr. Alexander is the first name that came to mind. We've got a sample of the murderer's DNA and we'll get back to you if we get a hit."

"Mr. Alexanders DNA is already linked into the CODIS system so there should be no issue there," says Lieutenant Towns. "Just download it and call me back when you get that hit, I know it's him."

As the police sit back and wait for the DNA sample to come back Lieutenant Towns informs Sergeant Hall of the possible new developments in the case and with all the publicity the case has garnered they believe that it will only be a matter of time before their suspect is captured. Back in room 109 of the rundown Kensington Motel, Michael and Cheryl are drinking and watching the updates on the news reports and drowning their sorrows in scotch.

"Man," says Michael. "What did I do to deserve this shit, my life is down the toilet now. If they catch me I'm done." Cheryl doesn't really comment but just continues to drink and pauses before speaking.

"Oh," says Michael. "You'll never guess who I ran into last night, none other than Coretta James." "Coretta James," says Cheryl. "Where did you see her?"

"A spot in South Central called The Hole in The Wall, he states, talk about the last person I expected to see .She still looks exactly the same."

"Yeah," says Cheryl. "The face of a supermodel with a heart full of mud. I don't think that woman cares for anyone or anything other than herself. Did she try to seduce you again." Michael just holds his head down and doesn't say anything, Cheryl just stares at him.

"Michael you didn't," says Cheryl. "I know you didn't sleep with Coretta James again." He doesn't say anything again and just looks away. Cheryl just looks away in disgust.

"After all this woman has done to you, she says, how could you do it."

"I blame it on the alcohol," says Michael. "I was good and toasted."

"Yea, don't use that as an excuse," says Cheryl. "There shouldn't be enough alcohol in the world to make you fuck

Coretta James again." Michael and Cheryl continue to drink and talk and eventually the two of them fall asleep across the twin bed and they leave the television on all night as they slumber. The following morning Cheryl wakes up under the covers of the twin bed in Michael's arms totally nude and not remembering how her clothes came off although her arms are wrapped totally around Michael. She lifts up the cover and sees the nude Michael and from smell of things and from the look of the bed she can put two and two together. She doesn't totally know what to believe in regards to Michael and she tries to pull away from him in the bed and get out of the room and do some thinking. As she gets out of the small twin bed she hears a loud rap at the door that makes her jump.

"Oh they found us," says Cheryl.

"Micheal you in there?" asks the voice. "Wake your ass up." The voice sounds familiar to Cheryl who looks through the window forgetting she is naked.

"Donald," says Cheryl. "Is that you." Donald sees Cheryl through the window with no clothes on.

"Shit," says Donald as Cheryl realizes her body is exposed.

"Michael told me this was his room," says Donald, what you doing in there buck necket. I knew you were fine girl but damn, and where's Michael anyway." Cheryl puts on a robe and opens the door and points to Michael on the bed. Donald looks back at Cheryl in amazement.

"It's not what it seems," says Cheryl. "We got drunk and passed out."

"Yea right," says Donald, that explains sleeping that doesn't explain being necket, I guess your clothes got drunk and went to sleep in the other room by themselves, hell ya'll grown and you don't owe me no explanation." As Donald talks the news is still going and the newscaster states that another woman was killed last night at 10pm and the DNA matches that of Michael Alexander making this his eight victim. Cheryl screams with joy and Donald doesn't know what is going on.

"Have you lost your damn mind Cheryl," says Donald, why in the world would you be so happy." "What time did you meet Michael last night Donald," asks Cheryl.

"7:30," says Donald, and he ran out at about 8."

"And it was no later than 8:30 when he got here," says Cheryl. "And he never left, so if he never left how could he kill a woman at 10pm,it's not possible."

"Yeah that's right," says Donald, I already knew that Michael didn't do those things he was being accused of."

"But I don't know how we're going to beat that DNA," says Cheryl. "The DNA doesn't lie."

"Well it's lying now," says Donald, cause my boy Michael ain't no pervert and the only way he would kill somebody is if they were messing with him or his family."

"Yeah," says Cheryl. "Well something is going on, maybe now that we know he didn't kill that girl last night he can turn himself in and we can prove that he didn't do the rest of those crimes."

"Are you crazy?" asks Donald. "If he turns himself in they will charge him with every crime since the Kennedy

Assassination, no, we got to find another way." As the two of them speak Michael arises from his drunken slumber and is surprised to see Donald in the room.

"So you heard me last night when I said room 109?" asks Michael. "I was kinda in a hurry."

"Yeah," says Donald, and when I got home and saw the news I understood why, you've been a busy man the last few months they say."

"Well what they say is wrong," says Michael. "They got me seriously confused with someone."

"Well while you were sleeping you killed another woman," says Cheryl. They say it happened around 10pm with a perfect DNA match, funny thing was I could have sworn that you were drinking scotch with me all last night."

"Yeah," says Donald, drinking scotch and fucking too." Cheryl has an embarrassed look on her face. As Michael Cheryl and Donald continue to talk, police in the area are investigating several sightings of Michael in the skid row area of LA. They believe that after all the sightings that he may actually be hiding out in the area.

"We talked to several people in the club Manhattan and the proprietor at the liquor store and they all believe that Mr. Alexander was in the area last night," says a detective on the search, but I know he wouldn't be dumb enough to still be in the area."

"Well the next place we need to check is the Kensington on Adams," says another Detective, that's a piece of shit but you never know. I'm headed over there now to see what I can find."

CHAPTER 23

A CLOSE CALL

The mad search continues for Michael and Cheryl as around the country Michael's picture and alleged crimes are broadcasted everywhere. In Alabama, Michael's daughter Brittany is home for a teacher's day off and the young girl is watching television and enjoying a sandwich when her father's image is broadcast across the screen and she quickly runs and calls her grandmother.

"Granny," says Brittany, daddy and Auntie Cheryl are on the TV."

"Girl what are you talking about," says Michael's mother, your daddy must be really prospering out there in LA."As she looks at the TV and sees her sons plight she is overcome with emotion.

"See Granny," says Brittany, daddy is in trouble." Michael's mother instantly turns off the television.

"Come on honey, she says, come and help Granny in the back."

"But Granny," says Brittany, what about Daddy and Aunt Cheryl." Granny stops talking and takes the little girl in the back and then grabs her cellphone and tries to reach Michael with no success. Back in room 109 of the Kensington, Donald decides to walk to the ice machine and notices the police presence at the front desk and he overhears them asking about Michael and runs back into the room. There's a police officer at the front asking the attendant if he has seen Michael and Cheryl and the attendant Sam doesn't recognize Michael but says he thinks Cheryl is the woman in room 109 and that she is really a fine woman. The officers walk around to the room and a woman comes to the door that looks nothing like Cheryl, and, as the officers enter the room, Michael, Cheryl and Donald look on from a distance outside the room from across the lot.

"Ma'am, how long have you been in this room," says the officer, did you purchase it."

"No," says the woman, a friend got it for me for a couple of nights and I am just here hanging out for a couple of days. " The officer pulls out a picture of Cheryl and Michael and asks the woman if she recognizes either picture.

"No," says the woman, I'm a working girl and I just needed a spot to chill out for a few days."

"The man working the front desk says this woman paid for this room," says the officer showing the woman a picture of Cheryl, "you sure you don't know her."

"I'm sure," says the woman, Sam doesn't know his elbow from his asshole. You officers are welcome to come in and look around." The officers look inside the room and then look around the parking lot and decide that there is nothing there.

"Thank you ma'am for your time," says the officer, let's go." Sam see's the officers start to leave and they stop in front of his office.

"Sir, says one of the officers, we're gonna need a copy of your video of the office and the parking lot for the last two days," says the officer.

"What video," says Sam the attendant, as far as I know we don't have a video, if you call the number on the front of the building it goes directly to the owner and you can ask him but as far as I know we don't have surveillance." The officers take off and Michael, Cheryl and Donald come out from their hideaway and head back to the room. Michael has on only his underwear and Cheryl has on a small gown with nothing on under it. Donald is admiring Cheryl in her very short gown with her incredible body.

"Girl when they was passing out body you stepped in line twice," says Donald, black women are amazing."

"Thank you, I guess," says Cheryl. "Let's get back in this room." Donald had grabbed a woman walking outside the room and promised to give her $100 dollars to pretend to live there and the woman played the role like a soldier. Cheryl opens the room and finds the woman standing inside looking like she needs a fix.

"Look honey," says Cheryl. "Here's two hundred dollars and you can stay in this room for the next two nights." Michael and Cheryl know that they need to move before the police check again.

"Look," says Donald, you guys can come to my spot, it's only five minutes up the road and I have two bedrooms and you can lay low until you figure out what you're going to do next."

"Solid," says Michael. "Let's move." Michael and Cheryl grab their things from the room and they head for Donald's residence which is only a short drive from the Motel. Upon entering into Donald's complex, Michael notices an unmarked car sitting right in front of where Donald lives and they seem to be monitoring his residence.

"That's an unmarked police car," says Michael. "How do they know about you."

"You sure that's a police car?" asks Donald. "There are no marks of any kind."

"That's what unmarked means Donald," says Michael. "They try to disguise it so they can catch you off guard. I remember that Detective Dana Andrews drove a car like that, he went to Jamaica with me to get the guys that killed my wife and he drove a car just like that. They have been checking my background so they know all my friends and relatives by now." Cheryl starts to tremble and Michael puts his arm around her.

"I would tell you to give yourself up but you would still get aiding and abetting a fugitive," says Michael. "I watch a lot of Law and Order. We better stick together till we find out what's really going on."

"Let's get out of here," says Donald.

"And go where?" asks Cheryl.

"Anywhere but here," says Michael. "Let's move." Cheryl is in the driver's seat of the rental and turns around and exits the complex and the three of them have nothing to do but drive around and contemplate their next move.

CHAPTER 24

MEDIA BLITZ

Meanwhile the SOPD have called a news conference to update the public on the manhunt for Michael Alexander. Sergeant Hall conducts the news conference surrounded by other city officials and attended by all the major news services both local and national. Sergeant Hall speaks from the podium.

"I'm Sergeant Dewayne Hall of the Sherman Oaks Police Dept. and I am the lead Detective assigned to this case, he says, we have unprecedented manpower and equipment assigned to this case. We have several sightings of the fugitives and we are confident that it will be only a matter of time before we apprehend them. Mr. Alexander is to be considered armed and dangerous. For now we don't have any more information. That's all for now." The parking lot full of reporters tries to ask questions as the Sergeant tries to leave.

"Sergeant Hall, Sergeant Hall, Sergeant," yells the reporters. One female reporter manages to get a question in.

"Sergeant, who tipped the fugitive off that he was about to be arrested?" asks the reporter.

"Well we believe the fugitive's Attorney overheard some Detectives speaking in the precinct," says Sergeant Hall. "And she obviously advised him to run."

"And is it true that the woman in question is Cheryl Bolling?" asks the reporter. "And she is the one that drove Mr. Alexander from the precinct and that she is the Attorney you are referring to?"

"That is correct," says Sergeant Hall as he hurries away avoiding any more questions from the reporters.

Meanwhile Michael, Cheryl and Donald have parked at an electronics store.

"Okay guys," says Michael. "We need a burner phone cause if we try and use our own cell phones they can track us immediately. Donald you have to go buy them."

"Why me?" asks Donald.

"Because our face is all over the news and we will be recognized instantly," says Michael. "But no one really knows that you are with us and you can be incognegro."

"Funny," says Donald. "I need some money." Michael gives Donald the money and Donald exits the car and heads inside and speaks to the attendant.

"Hey Captain," says Donald, I need to purchase three burner phones."

"Three?" says the salesperson, why three?" asks the salesperson.

"That's none of your damn business," says Donald, do you have them or not?"

"I got 'em," says the salesperson."

"Then hook um up, Donald says, how much for three."
The salesman gives Donald the price and after being paid he
starts to connect the burner phones. As Donald waits inside
for the burner phones Michael and Cheryl nervously wait for
him to finish and finally, after what seems like forever Donald
comes out with the three burner phones. Michael turns on his
old phone for a second because he needs a phone number.

"They can track that phone as soon as you turn it on," says
Donald, turn it off Mike."

"I need a number," says Michael. "As soon as I get this
number take off." Michael retrieves the number from the
phone and Cheryl takes off out of the parking lot. The officers
monitoring Michael's phone get a hit as soon as it turns on
but they lose it as Michael turns it off. They do have an idea of
the area that he is in because the tower that the phone pinged
is near by. Police then canvas the area but the fugitives are
nowhere to be found. Michael opens the burner phone and
dials a number.

"Coretta James please," says Michael to the person on the
other end of the phone, I need to speak to Coretta."

"This is Coretta Michael," says Correta. "How are you
sir, you are a very popular man these days. Rape, murder
and sodomy, Michael you have been a busy man, sloppy
though, you left a lot of evidence behind. Why didn't you use
a condom, you may as well have called the police while you
were there and just said come and get me."

"I didn't do that shit," says Michael. "I am being framed."

"By who," says Correta. "You mean to tell me that someone is walking around with a large amount of your sperm. I know you like spreading yourself around but that's a bit much don't you think."

"I can't explain it," says Michael. "But I didn't do any of that stuff."

"I believe you Michael," says Correta. "I never doubted you, that stuff is just not you. When I heard Anal penetration from my police contact, I knew it wasn't you. What can I do for you Mr. Alexander?"

"I need somewhere to lay low," says Michael. "Until I can get this stuff squared away."

"Can you get to the Staple Center?" asks Coretta. "I'm close by there now."

"We can be there in ten minutes," says Michael," what part do you want us to meet you at."

"Right in front," says Correta. "We'll be there waiting." Cheryl hits the 10 freeway believing that it is better to drive the freeway than the streets. The Staple center is 12 minutes away according to GPS. "Coretta James," says Cheryl. "How do you have contact with Coretta James."

"I thought I told you I ran into her the other night at the spot," says Michael.

"Yeah but you didn't tell me you had her number," says Cheryl. "And you talked mighty chummy with her." Cheryl looks across the seat at Michael and he looks down in guilt.

"I still can't believe it, Michael," says Cheryl while driving and staring, you fucked Coretta James, after all she did to you and your family, how could you. She killed your wife Michael, well, say something."

"There's nothing I can say," says Michael. "I was drunk and....look what's done is done. Now I'm glad I did because she has the connections to make us disappear, for good if necessary."

"As fine as Coretta James is, I couldn't have turned that pussy down either," says Donald, I don't care how sick she is."

"Shut up Donald," says Cheryl. "Nobody asked your opinion. I hope you don't believe you can trust Coretta Michael, that bitch is only loyal to herself." Michael, Cheryl and Donald pull up to the Staple Center and see Coretta's stretch Mercedes Limousine parked out front of the Staple Center.

"Park that car somewhere in one of the parking zones and get in," says Correta. "And call someone to come pick it up."

"I'll call my cousin," says Cheryl. "He rented the car for me anyway." The Limousine takes off and heads for one of Coretta's many houses.

"Cheryl Bolling," says Correta. "It's been quite a while. It's a pleasure to see you again."

"I can't say I feel the same way," Cheryl says. "I thought you'd be buried at the bottom of the ocean by now."

"Thought or hoped?" asks Coretta.

"Both," says Cheryl.

"Ladies please, "says Michael."

"Cheryl Bolling," says Correta. "Always ready to come to her ex best friends husband Michael's rescue. What friend would put her own life on the line for a man like that. You fucked him yet?" Cheryl doesn't say anything as Coretta looks on in amazement.

"You have fucked him," says Correta. "Michael Alexander you're a busy man. That thing gonna fall off one day." Coretta won't stop talking.

"That Dick was good wasn't it Cheryl," says Correta. "Let's see, he is your ex husbands best friend, you are his daughters Godmother, you crossed every line possible."

"Talk about the pot calling the kettle black," says Cheryl. "A skank bitch like you can't talk about nobody."

"How bout if this skank bitch stops the car and whup your ass?" asks Coretta. "You don't want none of this."

"You gotta bring some ass to get some ass," says Cheryl.

"Ladies please, Michael says, Cheryl call your cousin and tell him to pick up that car so it can't be traced back to you." Donald thinks out loud, "All I need is a bag of popcorn" ,says Donald smirking.

"Yea Cheryl," says Correta. "make sure you do what Michael says or you won't get no more of that good loving." Cheryl ignores Coretta for the moment and does call her cousin so that he can pick up the rental. Her cousin inquires about her whereabouts and if she is ok and goes about the task of retrieving the rental car. After Cheryl hangs up the phone she sits back in the Limo and tries to ignore Coretta. Coretta looks on the side of the Limo where Cheryl is and notices that Cheryl doesn't have on much at all in the way of clothes.

"I thought we were having fish for dinner," says Correta. "But now I see where that smell is coming from."

Nobody speaks and Michael just stares at Coretta.

CHAPTER 25

THE HIDEOUT

Coretta instructs her driver to drive into the Hollywood Hills and they go down several winding roads and end at a property off the grid, a large ranch style home in a very secluded area and with a large gate at the front.

"Wow, I've never been back here," says Michael. "This is what I call secluded."

"Not many people have," says Correta. "I bought this house from an old gay white actor whom I will not name. I think they had their private shindigs back here. There's 5000 sq. ft, 5 bedrooms and four baths and four showers." When Coretta mentions the four showers she looks at Cheryl.

"Michael, here's the key and the alarm code," says Correta. "There should be food but if you need anything call me. I've got to leave right now, business to attend to." Coretta instructs her driver to drive out the gates and Michael opens the residence and finds a well furnished abode with wood floors and all the amenities of home. Cheryl looks around and scouts out the bedrooms and bathrooms and decides to go freshen up as Michael and Donald kind of take a deep breath as they feel they can relax for a second.

"What a day," says Michael as he lounges on the charcoal grey swirl sofa, I feel like I can exhale for a moment."

"Just a moment," says Donald, we still have a lot to figure out."

"Yeah but I'm gonna figure that out after I take a nap," says Michael who falls asleep right there on the sofa.

Back at the SOPD Lieutenant Towns is taking calls at her desk when an Officer comes in with the fingerprint results from the crime scenes relating to Michael Alexander. As Lieutenant Towns ends her phone call the officer hands her the fingerprint analysis.

"Here are the fingerprint results from that sick Michael Alexander," says the officer, this should pretty much seal his coffin." Lieutenant Towns excitedly opens the envelope and looks at the results and stops talking.

"Is something wrong Lieutenant?" asks the officer. "You ok?"

"Of course I am," says Lieutenant Towns. "Has anybody else seen this."

"No," says the officer. "Is there anything else you need from me?"

"No," says Lieutenant Towns. "That will be all, this is just what we needed to make our case stick, thank you officer." Lieutenant Towns takes the fingerprint information and puts it in her drawer and goes about the rest of her business of trying to get enough evidence to convict Michael. Back at the hideout in Hollywood Hills Cheryl has cleaned up and lays across the bed in one of the bedrooms and Michael is still fast asleep on the sofa while Donald sits back and watches the news reports about Michael and Cheryl, mostly about Michael. He decides to go into the room where Cheryl is laying across the bed and tries to pick her brain.

"So what do you think is really going on?" asks Donald. "Michael has his faults but the kind of stuff they say that he is doing doesn't make any sense. I've known Mike forever and I have never known him to do anything like this, it just doesn't make sense."

"I know," says Cheryl. "Why would he put himself out like that. The Michael I know would never do this and he would definitely not be bold enough to show his face on the camera like that and pose, it doesn't make any sense. But that DNA evidence is hard to fight."

"Well this is a beautiful area, a beautiful house," says Donald, I love the isolation, I'm going to sit out on the patio and enjoy the view and the breeze, maybe you should relax and enjoy the ambiance as best as you can."

"Yeah," says Cheryl. "I'm going to enjoy the rest of the evening and relax." As Donald goes outside on the patio Cheryl undresses and walks into the living room area where Michael is sleeping and starts kissing on him. Michael wakes up and sees Cheryl's beautiful nude body standing over him and pauses for a second.

"Last night we were drunk and didn't know what we were doing," says Cheryl. "I'm fully awake now Michael." He looks up from his slumber.

"Where is Donald?" asks Michael. "He's gonna see us." Cheryl grabs Michael's hand and leads him to a bedroom down the hall and he takes off his clothes and immediately starts to sex Cheryl. Michael does her doggy style from the back and then turns her over and does it missionary and it is so intense that Cheryl's head falls off the bed but her lower body is still in the bed and Michael continues to give it to her with her head on the floor and the rest of her body in the bed. They both release their pressure and afterwards Cheryl wants to sleep with Michael for the rest of the night. "Let me lay in your arms all night Mike, she says, I don't want to be alone."

"No," says Michael. "Donald is going to be checking the rooms and you know how nosy he is. We got plenty of time to be together." At that Cheryl grabs a sheet from the bed and sneaks back to her room as Donald is still on the patio. Michael is really tired now and immediately falls back to sleep.

CHAPTER 26

THE SET UP

As Michael and Cheryl have enjoyed their night and Donald somewhat enjoys the hideaway a call comes in to the SOPD and the caller asks to speak to Sergeant Hall. Sergeant Hall answers the call.

"Is this Sergeant Hall?" asks the voice. "Sergeant Dwayne Hall?"

"Yes it is," says the Sergeant. "To whom am I speaking?"

"Is there a reward for Michael Alexander yet?" asks the voice. "I can give him to you on a silver platter."

"Are you trying to blackmail the police? asks Sergeant Hall. "You can do some serious time for blackmail." As Sergeant Hall speaks he whispers to his fellow officers to trace the call.

"You're wasting your time trying to trace me," says the voice, announce a $1 million dollar reward and I will hand Michael Alexander to you on a silver platter." The caller hangs up immediately. "Did you get a fix on the call?" asks Sergeant Hall. "No," says the officer," he hung up too fast." Sergeant Hall immediately goes to the office of the Precinct Captain Joseph Hardy and makes a request for a ransom.

"Captain Hardy? asks Sergeant Hall. "Why don't we come up with a ransom big enough to get someone to talk them out of hiding?"

"Well I do believe that a ransom is necessary," says the Captain, maybe $60,000 or even $75,000 I could easily justify."

"How about $1 million," says Sergeant Hall, let's smoke this clown out."

"A million," says Captain Hardy, do you know what a million dollars would do to our budget?" Sergeant Hall walks over to the window.

"Captain, he says, you see all those reporters camped outside. Do you see the new vans that have been posted up outside since this started, I can't even walk out the door without being bombarded with questions. We haven't had anything this big in LA County since the OJ trial. I just got a call from someone that promised me that they can deliver Michael Alexander on a silver platter."

"And you believe him?" asks Captain Hardy.

"I don't know if I believe him or not but we allow people to remain anonymous when they provide info to the police all the time so what do we have to lose. We don't pay the money until we have apprehended the suspect anyway so there's really no risk. But if this person is telling the truth and we bag this perp then we will be the talk of the town. Donations and donors will come pouring in from near and far and the main thing is we need to get this man off the streets before another woman ends up dead."

"Make the announcement," says Captain Hardy, I will find the money." Captain Hardy, a 6ft stocky 50 year old white man has saw his share of buzz around the police but nothing to the extent of this. As Captain Hardy makes a few calls Sergeant Hall and Lieutenant Towns hold an impromptu news conference as the press rushes forward to see what the news is. Sergeant Hall yells out.

"Can I have everyone's attention please, he yells, I have an announcement, the SOPD would like to announce that one million dollars will be paid for anyone who knows the location and whereabouts of Michael Alexander and if that information leads to his capture and conviction. Remember you can remain anonymous." The crowd of reporters start to buzz but the officers take no questions and rush back into the precinct. Sergeant Hall makes it known to all the officers on duty that if any calls come through for him patch them in immediately. Meanwhile, back at their hideaway Donald is watching the news while Michael and Cheryl try to relax and try to put the day's events behind them. A newsflash comes across interrupting whatever Donald is thinking. At the bottom of the screen he sees in bold letters" One million dollars is being offered for the arrest and conviction of Michael Alexander and you can remain anonymous'.

"Oh no," says Donald, the shit done hit the fan." Donald walks in where Michael is sleeping.

"Michael wake your ass up," says Donald, Cheryl you need to come and see this." Cheryl runs in the room and

Michael arises from his slumber. Cheryl reads the caption at the bottom of the page and starts to panic. Michael also reads.

"Oh no," says Michael. "I'm fucked."

"No more than you were before," says Donald, you know we won't turn you in and the only other person that knows where you are is Coretta, I guess we are about to find out where her loyalties lie. Now that I think about it I could use that million dollars."

"Not funny," says Michael loudly. He knows the betrayal from Coretta's past and starts to wonder himself.

"Coretta's only loyalties are to Coretta," says Cheryl.

"Yea," says Michael. "But Coretta is a billionaire,$1 million dollars is a drop in the bucket to her." In the meantime Sergeant Hall sits around the station during the evening hoping that the caller that called earlier would call back, but after sitting for several hours he begins to believe that the earlier call was a prank call and he begins to walk out of the door when he hears the phone ring.

"Sergeant Hall," says the officer, this is for you." "Send it to my office," says the Sergeant. He goes to his office and answers. "This is Sergeant Hall."

"I will have Mr. Alexander tomorrow at noon," says the caller, how do I collect the money?"

"Don't worry," says Sergeant Hall, you give me Michael Alexander and I will get you the money, I can deposit it into your bank account."

"No," says the caller, I want cash only. I will provide the place to put the money and I will call you in the morning with the place." The caller hangs up and Sergeant Hall reports to Captain Hardy.

"Well the potential informant called back Captain," says Sergeant Hall, now it's a just a matter of us waiting for that next phone call, and Captain, did we get the funds together?"

"I will have it all together in the morning," says Captain Hardy, don't worry about the funds just get this guy off the streets." That night Michael gets a good night's sleep even with all the stuff going on around him. Cheryl doesn't sleep well because she has never been in trouble with the law before.

CHAPTER 27

NOWHERE TO RUN

The next morning Coretta comes over at 8am with breakfast for everyone, even Cheryl, and the four of them enjoy their food and have some sense of normalcy for a moment.

"Everyone can just lay low here for the time being," says Correta. "Michael we're going to probably change your identity and get you to a country that has no extradition treaty with the US."

"I can't clear my name if I run," says Michael. "I don't want to run."

"You want a clear name or freedom, says Coretta, you stay here and some big brother gonna try to have you trimming his toe nails for the rest of your life. If you go where they won't send you back you can work on your good name from over there. Can't clear your name from jail handsome."

"I hate to agree with Coretta but she has a point," says Cheryl. "You stay here you'll be making license plates for the rest of your life." As Cheryl, Michael and Coretta talk Donald comes from one of the restroom wearing some brief underwear and walking through the room like he is alone, the girls just stare at him.

"Man can you go put some clothes on," says Michael. "Don't nobody want to see you walking around in your draws."

"Man, you're just jealous," says Donald, you just wish you had a body like this." Donald's 5ft 6in body is not in any kind of shape with no muscles to be found anywhere.

"No I don't," says Michael.

"Anyway, I got an appointment at 10am says Coretta, and I probably won't be done till about 3pm and I will bring a nice dinner, even for you Cheryl, and then we can talk more about our plans." Coretta leaves the room and gets in the Limo and talks to her driver.

"Ok Malcolm," says Correta. "Get me to my appointment."

"Boss lady," says Malcolm, you mind if I use the restroom before I go."

"Of course not," says Correta. "Take your time as we're in no real rush."

"Ok I'll be right back," says Malcolm. Malcolm is a 6ft 3 inch somewhat muscular black man who is not one of Coretta's regular drivers but she has learned to have some semblance of trust for him. When he enters the house Donald is changing his clothes and Cheryl is in the other room and Michael is in the front room by himself. Malcolm enters the front room and speaks to Michael.

"Mr. Alexander," says Malcolm, the boss lady said for me to pick you up at 11am while she is at her first appointment.

She has got her man ready to get your photos because you are going to need new passports to get out of the country, but just you."

"Okay," says Michael. "You said 11."

"Yes sir," says Malcolm exiting the residence. Malcolm jumps in the Limo and immediately takes off.

"That was quick," says Coretta.

"False alarm," says Malcolm. Back in the house Cheryl comes into to living room area after hearing voices.

"Who were you talking to Michael, she asks , that didn't sound like Donald."

"That was the Limo driver," says Michael. "I guess Coretta sent him in here to give me a message, he is going to pick me up at 11 and work on getting me a passport. Kind of a weird guy though."

"Well look who he's driving for, Cheryl adds, you know that's the first time I have ever known Coretta to allow someone to speak for her. Passports already, that lady can take care of business."

"She sure can, he states, look Cheryl, about what we did the other night and last night."

"Please Michael, I let you do that," she says, I have to admit I have always had a curiosity, curiosity satisfied, very much so." He just looks at the beautiful Cheryl and realizes that their relationship will never be the same. Back at the SOPD Sergeant Hall and Lieutenant Towns just wait for the call from the anonymous person that promised to give Michael up at noon but no one has called as of 10am. The officers just look at their watches and patiently await the call and until it comes they go over other cases that they are working on.

"Did we receive the fingerprint analysis from the crime scenes of Michael Alexander Lieutenant Towns, asks the Sergeant , they should be back by now."

"No we haven't received them yet," says Lieutenant Towns. "Let me follow up again." She runs to her office and makes some personal phone calls. At 10am Malcolm drops Coretta off at her appointment. Coretta likes for her drivers to stay in the area while she is in meetings but since she expects this meeting to last until 3pm so she doesn't monitor Malcolm so closely.

"Don't go too far away Malcolm in case the meeting ends a little early," she says.

"Okay boss lady, "says Malcolm. He drops off Coretta and heads directly back towards Hollywood Hills to pick up Michael at 11am. At 10:15 the call the officers have been waiting for comes into the station.

"I'll be at the front of Hollywood Park at noon," says the anonymous voice, have the money in a bag for me and I will cover my face to stay anonymous. I will be there at 12 noon and I will be in a Black Stretch Mercedes Limo." The caller hangs up and Sergeant Hall and Lieutenant Towns mobilize the SWAT team and get bulletproof vests and prepare as if they are taking down an Army instead of one potentially unarmed man. The officers canvas the area and make sure there are no civilians and they walk around the front of the park dumping trash as if they are employed by the park while the other Detectives just sit back and wait for Michael to appear. The officers have notified several news agencies that there will be a big arrest at noon but to keep a distance as there could be danger. The trap is set and the only thing left is for the mouse to appear. Back at the house it is 10:55 am and Michael looks outside and Coretta's Limo is already sitting and waiting. Cheryl only has some of the female clothes that she found in the closet and at this point she walks around in some shorts shorts and Michael stares in lust.

"Shit girl," says Donald coming from the other room, you walk outside right now and all the traffic will stop. You make a blind man want to see." Donald just goes on and Michael has to go.

"You sure you need to be going out, asks Cheryl, you probably need to lay low."

"Nobody can see me in that Limo," says Michael. "The windows are tinted and I will lay low."

"Yea and keep your eyes on that weird ass driver," says Donald, he may have eyes for you too."

"Oh boy," says Michael.

"Well it will be kind of lonely without you," says Cheryl.

"You won't be lonely baby," says Donald, I'm gonna keep your fine ass company. I will be your personal bodyguard and believe me I will guard that body." Michael and Cheryl laugh at Donald and Michael heads out the door towards the Limo. As he nears the car he is having second thoughts.

"Maybe I should just stay here, he says, as the driver Malcolm holds open the door, discretion can be the better part of valor." Malcolm thinks quick.

"This is the only day we can do it," says Malcolm slyly, he is only in town today and then he has to move on." Michael reluctantly gets in the car and it takes off. Back at Coretta's appointment she has to leave her meeting for a moment to get something from her car and she notices that her Limo is nowhere around. She calls Malcolm to bring the Limo back so that she can retrieve her papers but he doesn't answer. The phone just rings. In the Limo Michael notices the phone ringing and asks Malcolm about it.

"Why you not answering the phone?" asks Michael. Malcolm doesn't answer because of course he knows the call is coming from Coretta. On the other end Coretta is very upset,

"He won't be driving for me again, she says angrily, he knows I don't play this shit." She goes back inside quite annoyed while Michael and the driver head towards his destiny with the police. As Michael and the Limo driver head up the 101 freeway Michael thinks that it is odd that they are going towards the Valley because he would expect to have fake passports made downtown LA.

"Hey man where we going ,he asks as the Limo driver exits on the Hollywood park exit, what we going to Hollywood Park for." The Limo driver is bald and Michael talks about his head.

"Hey man anybody ever told you your head looks like a Dick?" asks Michael. "Hey man what you up to, take me back." Michael knows he's in trouble and as the car slows down entering the park. He jumps from the car and takes off and almost as soon as he hits the ground the police are on top of him yelling.

"Get on the ground, get on the ground, yells the police, put your hands behind your head." The police lift Michael up off the ground and Lieutenant Towns rushes towards him as Sergeant Hall trails behind, "Michael Alexander, you are under arrest for Murder, rape and sodomy, You have the right to remain silent and if you give up the right to remain silent, anything you say can and will be used against you in a court of law, you have the right to an Attorney and if you cannot afford an Attorney one will be appointed for you, do you understand your rights, Mr. Alexander," says Lieutenant Towns rudely.

"Fuck you," says Michael. Sergeant Hall grabs Michael by the collar.

"You better watch your mouth" says the Sergeant.

CHAPTER 28

LOCK UP

Reporters and news people come to the front of the car and snap Michael's picture as he holds his head down in the backseat of the police car. The reporters fire question after question at him.

"Mr. Alexander, did you rape those women," says one reporter, did you murder those women, Mr. Alexander do you have anything to say for yourself.

"Mr. Alexander are you a rapist, are you a murderer, you're a sick man, "and many other chants from the crowd. Sergeant Hall confronts Malcolm who continues to hide his face so he can't be seen by the reporters. He gives Malcolm a bag and Malcolm asks for a ride to his residence and the Sergeant assigns a Detective to drive him through the crowd to his home in Van Nuys and soon the detective drops Malcolm off at home. Malcolm just leaves Coretta's Limo sitting on the curb with the doors wide open. Sergeant Hall and Lieutenant Towns jump into the backseat with Michael and head for LA County jail to book their new celebrity prisoner into jail. News of Michaels arrest quickly spreads across Southern California and across the nation. Local news Channels interrupt their regular scheduled programming to report the fact that Michael Alexander, the notorious murderer and rapist has been arrested. Back at Coretta's board meeting the news of the arrest is shown on the television in the boardroom, her Limo is also shown with the doors wide open as Michael is being arrested and she immediately walks out of the meeting and calls Malcolm who of course can't answer the phone. Back at the house in Hollywood Hills Cheryl screams loudly and Donald runs in the room.

"I haven't made a woman scream that loud in years," jokes Donald. Cheryl doesn't speak but just points at the TV. Donald sees the Limo and Michael being arrested and comes to his own conclusions.

"I knew it was something up with that Limo driver, he says , he looked at Michael real weird when they picked us up at the Staples Center."

"What are we going to do now Donald, asks Cheryl, Michael pretends to be tough but he can't handle jail."

"Michael ain't no pushover," says Donald, he will figure it out."

"We gotta get him out Donald, yells Cheryl frantically, we gotta get him out."

"Get him out how," says Donald, this ain't the movies."

"That bitch Coretta," says Cheryl. "She set this up."

"Coretta, what did Coretta do?" asks Donald. "I don't believe that. The way she looks at Michael, there's something really deep there. If that was the case they would be here arresting us too. It was that Limo driver." Back in Alabama Michael's mother has been watching CNN and has seen her son being arrested and t she tries to shield her granddaughter from the television, but she knows that she can only do that for so long. Meanwhile Malcolm's police Uber ride has pulled up in front of his apartment and he exits the police car and heads for his apartment 1 million dollars richer. Malcolm enters his apartment and smiles broadly and immediately starts to count his ill gotten money. As he continues to count he looks up and sees a man standing right in front of him holding a gun with a silencer and pointed directly at him and he stands up in fear and disbelief.

"You," says Malcolm, it's not possible, how can this this be possible. Please, begs Malcolm, don't kill me."

"You know what they say motherfucker," says the voice, all money ain't good money." With that the man shoots Malcolm twice and he drops to the floor dead. The man grabs the bag full of money and exits out the fire escape side of Malcolm's apartment and jumps in his car and slowly drives off. Back at Hollywood Hills Donald and Cheryl sit around in a state of disbelief as Coretta pulls up in the back seat of her royal blue Mercedes Sedan driven by her regular driver and she is in a very somber mood. Coretta walks into the home in tears as her Limo driver helps her to her seat. Cheryl is initially furious with Coretta but she sees the genuine compassion that she shows over Michael's arrest and realizes that she could not have played a part in Michael's demise.

"She cried all the way here," says the driver, I've never seen her like this before."

"What am I going to tell my son?" asks Coretta. "What am I gonna do."

"What son," asks Cheryl."

"I'm not sure what she means," says the driver, as far as I know she has no kids." Cheryl, despite her disdain for Coretta sits with her on the edge of the chair and tries to console her and the two women share a hug of unity in wanting to see Michael free.

"I'll make sure we retrieve your other car," says the driver, I'll be back shortly boss lady." While the mood is somber Michael arrives at the LA county jail to be booked and fingerprinted and put in the general population. As he arrives at the jail the media outlets are still hounding him and calling him names and this continues until he disappears into the jail area. After Michael is brought in he has to give next of kin and then his pockets are searched and his belts and shoestrings are removed and he is fingerprinted and photographed with a number next to his head. Since he is a felony prisoner he will be dressed in a jumpsuit and moved directly to general population. As he moves from one correction officer to another they all make him do different demeaning tasks and as Michael goes through the last step before going up to the seventh floor general population one officer makes him strip and asks him to spread his butt cheeks.

"You gay or something?" asks Michael. "What the hell am I gonna hide in my butt?"

"Just shut up and do what you told," says the officer, or you gonna have problems." Michael refuses to comply and gets up and grabs his clothes.

"I'm gonna ask you one more time to obey my command," says the officer, if you don't you're mine."

"Go fuck yourself," says Michael. "You took my life but you not gonna take my dignity." The officer moves forward to strike Michael and a fellow officer stops him.

"What you doing man, asks a Senior officer, the man just got here and you about to whip his ass already."

"He got to follow the rules," says the officer, or he gonna get his skull cracked."

"Pick your clothes up son and put them on and then line up against the wall so we can take you to your pod," says the senior officer to Michael. Michael is lined up and marched up to the felony pod on the seventh floor and then he walks in with the rest of the new people and tries to find a place to sleep. Crips, bloods, Mexican gangs and skinheads all occupy the pod. Michael tries to look tough as he walks around trying to find a bunk.

"You got to sleep over here brother," says another inmate, that area is for the bloods."

"How you know I ain't no blood?" asks Michael. "You see my red eyes."

"Funny," says the inmate, you ain't no blood or crip, you just a regular brother like me. The bunk on the bottom is empty, just stay in your lane around here and you will be fine."

"I'm Michael Alexander," says Michael. "What's your name brother."

"Carlton Thomas," says the inmate, what you are in for."

"Murder," says Michael. "Rape, you name it."

"You don't seem like that type," says Carlton the inmate. "You seem too clean cut." Carlton is a 50 something year old black man about 6ft 1 inches tall with a dark complexion and he is slender with a beard.

"We all were clean cut at one time," says Michael. "But you're right, I didn't do it. A bunch of women have been getting raped around Southern California and some have been killed and they say I did it, a woman identified me, they say my DNA was found at the scene of all the rapes and murders and I have no idea how that can be possible."

"The only way that's possible is if you did or unless you have a twin brother," says Carlton. "Other than that it had to be you."

"Well I don't have a twin," says Michael. "And it still wasn't me."

"Well, you can have that bunk," says Carlton. "I'm going to be a trustee soon so I will be living in the trustee quarters." The inmates are playing a lot of spades and dominoes and there is one TV in the pod for everyone to watch and the area inside looks like a large dorm room except everyone is dressed in blue jumpsuits.

CHAPTER 29

THE BRIBE

While Michael tries to get adjusted to his new surroundings Lieutenant Towns goes to speak to the LA County DA about evidence against Michael. The DA is an attractive young white female by the name of Sandra Cox with long blonde hair and a very nice body but very strict about the law. Lieutenant Towns goes to Ms. Cox office and enters the office.

"Hi Ms. Cox, she says , thank you for seeing me on such short notice.

"No problem, and please call me Sandra. I want to congratulate you on your big arrest, getting that maniac off the streets was a real coup."

"Yeah," says Lieutenant Towns. "We may have a bit of a problem. The fingerprints don't match Mr. Alexander's fingerprints. Although Mr. Alexander's DNA is present at every crime scene, his fingerprints are not present at any crime scene."

"Maybe he just cleaned up the scene," says Sandra Cox. "Maybe he wiped up well."

"Well it doesn't make sense that he left semen all over the place," says Lieutenant Towns. "And he cleaned up his prints. And besides, we found prints at every crime scene, the same prints but none of them match Mr. Alexander."

"Who do they match"?, asks Ms. Cox.

"Nobody that has ever been arrested," says Lieutenant Towns. "At least not so far. It's really strange."

"Well we've got DNA," says Sandra Cox. "We've got an eyewitness and we have video evidence that definitely shows Mr. Alexander at the scene of the crimes, so we have enough. We just won't mention the fingerprint evidence. By the way, when do you interrogate him?"

"On my way to see him now," says Lieutenant Towns. "Can't wait to see the look on his face."

"Do me a big favor," says the DA. "Get me a confession."

"I will," says Lieutenant Towns. "I will." Lieutenant Towns exits the office and heads to the LA County Jail to interrogate Michael along with her partner Sergeant Hall.

Back in Hollywood Hills Coretta James goes into action to find a way to help Michael. Instead of her calling her Attorney she has other ideas in mind and she talks to Cheryl.

"I need to get in contact with that Detective that came to Jamaica with Michael when they were looking for us, what was his name, "asks Coretta.

"Dana Andrews," says Cheryl. "What do you have in mind."

"I'm going to make him an offer he can't refuse, Coretta says, did he get reinstated to the force."

"Yeah they finally took him back," says Cheryl. "He and I talk every now and then, Michael and him were like brothers."

"Can I have his phone number please?" asks Coretta. "He and I need to have a heart to heart." Coretta gets the number and calls Detective Andrews who immediately answers the phone.

"This is Dana Andrews," says Detective Andrews, how can I help you."

"Detective, this is Coretta James, do you remember me." Detective Andrews hesitates and groans.

"You're unforgettable, he adds, and it's Officer Andrews now thanks to you, after that fiasco in Jamaica I'm just a decorated pencil pusher. How did you get out of that fire anyway.?"

"We can talk about that later," says Correta. "Have you heard about Michael?"

"Of course, he says, you have to be living under a rock not to hear that. After all that trouble we went through with Stephen raping and killing those girls I can't believe he would do this."

"He didn't do it," says Correta. "Look, I'm texting you my address where I am now and I need you to be here in the next hour." Coretta hangs up the phone before Officer Andrews can answer and patiently waits for him to arrive.

"You forget he is still the police," says Cheryl. "And Donald and I are still wanted."

"That man would never tell on you," says Correta. "I'm going to test his devotion to Michael." As Coretta waits for

Officer Andrews to arrive Lieutenant Towns and Sergeant Hall
go to the interrogation room to try and get a confession out
of Michael. They bring in a bottle of water and Lieutenant
Towns is ready to go to war with Michael and Sergeant Hall
has to calm her down.

"Let's go get this perv," says Lieutenant Towns. "I'm gonna
be on his ass like stank on shit."

"If you go in there with an attitude like that we're not going
to get anywhere," says the Sergeant, calm down and don't take
it so personal."

"I never told you this," says Lieutenant Towns. "But my
sister was assaulted. That's why I became a police officer, to
weed out trash like this."

"I agree he is trash," says the Sergeant, but we must be
tactful." Sergeant Hall calmly walks into the interrogation
room with a bottle of water and asks Michael how he is doing
so far.

"I'm just peachy," says Michael. "How you think I'm doing.
All y'all want to do is lock up brothers."

"Brothers like you need to be locked up," says Lieutenant
Towns. "You just a piece of shit." Michael just stares at her.

"So it's gonna be like this, he says, when the last time you
had some Dick Lieutenant Towns." Lieutenant Towns scowls
and Sergeant Hall holds his hands up to tell her to relax and
he talks to Michael and tries to hand him a bottle of water.

"No thanks," says Michael. "I don't need any tokens from
you."

'Suit yourself," says Sergeant Hall, you do realize that you don't have to talk to us."

"I don't have anything to hide," says Michael. "I got truth on my side." As Michael prepares for his interrogation Officer Andrews arrives at Coretta James hideaway in Hollywood Hills and enters and he sees that Cheryl and Donald are also there.

"What an odd threesome," says Officer Andrews, I would have never thought in a thousand years you would be here. Ms. Bolling you have been a busy girl, running away with your client before he is arrested, now that takes balls, excuse the expression."

"Well," says Cheryl ,a girl gotta do what a girl gotta do."

"Yeah," says Officer Andrews, how do you know I won't arrest right now."

"Whatever," says Correta. "You love Michael as much as we do, I need you to help us get him out."

"Get him out, and just how do you expect me to do that, he asks, that's an impossible task."

"It's not like you are beyond doing what it takes to make things happen," says Correta. "So let's cut the bullshit. You know that I'm a billionaire right."

"I've heard the rumors, he says, you kind of flaunt your good fortune at times."

"Well my good fortune will become your good fortune if you get Michael out, she says, and there are fifty million reasons why you should help."

"So you're trying to bribe me into getting myself locked up with Michael," says Officer Andrews, and how am I supposed to get him out."

"That's your job to figure that out," says Correta. "Here, take this." Coretta hands Officer Andrews a package that he opens and looks inside of.

"There's one hundred thousand dollars in that bag," says Correta. "Use it to get whatever you need to help you out. I will give 50 million more when I see Michael, so figure something out." Officer Andrews doesn't even hesitate to take the money."

"How do you know I won't take this money and run," says Officer Andrews.

"Run where," says Correta. "I think you know the kind of person that I am from past experience, in other words I would find your ass and $100,000 would be the least of your problems. Now go, you're wasting time here talking to me." The Officer heads towards the door.

"You know you're strange, he says to Coretta, I remember when you were trying to kill Michael and now you seem desperate to save him, what's up with that."

"I have my reasons," says Correta. "And the time you're spending here asking me questions could be better spent helping Michael." With that the officer leaves and contemplates his next move and how or if he can possibly get Michael out of jail.

CHAPTER 30

INTERROGATION

Back in the interrogation room things are getting very tense as the two Detectives try unsuccessfully to get Michael to confess.

"You see that video right there, yells Sergeant

Hall, that's you coming out of that building at the exact same time of the assault, how the fuck do you explain that."

"You crooked ass cops probably doctored that video," says Michael. "You will do anything to lock a brother up."

"What about your DNA, shouts Lieutenant Towns, how did we doctor that up, brother."

Michael has no answer for that question.

"You know something Towns," says Michael. "You want my DNA in you don't you. I can see the way you look at me. Sorry, it ain't gonna happen, I don't like ugly women."

"Watch your mouth," says Sergeant Hall, don't you think you're already in enough trouble. Now, tell me how you're coming out of the victims homes posing for the cameras at the time of the rape and yet you say it wasn't you."

"I went to see your Mama in there," says Michael. "But the bitch was so fat both of us couldn't fit in the room." Sergeant Hall grabs Michael by the collar and throws him up against the wall.

"Don't forget you're on candid camera," says Michael. "There is nothing that you can do or say that will make me confess to something I didn't do it. You're wasting your time." With that the two Detectives call for the officers to take Michael back to his cell as Sergeant Hall has to restrain himself from striking Michael.

As Michael is escorted back to his cell Officer Andrews calls down to the LA County jail to the cell phone of the Corrections officer that handles the first floor where the holding cells are,

His name is Rodney Givhan.

"Givhan," says Officer Andrews as Rodney answers the phone, you heard about that inmate down there named Michael Alexander."

"Of course," says Givhan, everybody has heard that story. Bulldog Towns and Sergeant Hall are interrogating him now."

"Do me a favor," says Officer Andrews, put him in a holding cell on the first floor and don't send him back to the pod. Just say he is causing a problem or we want him in solitary or something. I also need you to meet with me in the morning after your shift."

"What's up Andrews,"?," says Givhan.

"I will tell you when I see you," says Officer Andrews, let me buy you breakfast at the Awful House in the morning, let's say 7:30. Take care of Mr. Alexander for me."

"Ok," says Givhan, and I will see you there in the morning because I'm usually starving when I get out of here and I can't turn down a free meal." Givhan of course has no idea what Officer Andrews wants but they have been tight for years so he follows his instructions. Right after his conversation with Officer Andrews, Givhan notices Michael Alexander being put in a holding cell and goes to speak to him.

"Mr. Alexander, I'm Officer Givhan and I am the floor supervisor for the night shift. How long did they keep you in that interrogation?."

"Four hours," says Michael. "Asking me them dumb ass questions trying to make me say I did something I didn't do."

"Well Officer Dana Andrews told me to look out for you so that's what I'm going to do. Did you eat yet? asks Givhan"

"Hell no," says Michael. "And I'm starving, did you say Dana Andrews, we go back a long way."

"Yeah, he asked me to take care of you, I'll get the trustees to bring you some food," says Givhan, the food we eat in our cafeteria is a lot better than that mess they serve the inmates. I'll have the trustees bring you a chicken sandwich with some fries, can you handle that."

"Yeah," says Michael. "Is there a Church service in jail, I know tomorrow is Sunday."

"Yeah," says Givhan, it starts at 10am, I'll put you on the list.'

"Thanks man," says Michael. "And thanks for the sandwich.

"No problem," says Givhan. The trustee drops off the sandwich and Michael unwraps the sandwich and sees that it is a roast beef sandwich instead of chicken and since he does not eat roast beef he still goes through the night hungry.

CHAPTER 31

FERGUSON

At 6:30 am the next morning Officer Givhan is preparing for the end of his shift and his replacement for the day shift Officer Glenn Ferguson comes in ready for the day. Officer Ferguson is a 6ft 4in. white ex Marine and ex skinhead with a heavily tattooed body and he loves to pit the white inmates against the blacks and hispanics. Ferguson is an instigator that is always inciting insurrection in the jail and pitting white inmates against blacks and showing the whites special favoritism.

"Givhan I heard we have a new prisoner by the name of Michael Alexander," says Ferguson, a murderer and a rapist, a real credit to his race. I came in early to make his acquaintance. A little birdy told me he was on the first floor."

"I'm sure he gonna love you Ferguson," says Givhan, all the prisoners love you."

"It must be my charming personality," says Ferguson," you know I treat them all the same." Givhan just stares at Ferguson and heads up front to check out. Immediately after Ferguson finishes checking in he opens the gate and goes towards the inmates cells and finds Michael sleeping and just stares at him with disdain.

"I'm going to make sure you have a pleasant stay rapist," says Ferguson to a sleeping Michael, I'm gonna enjoy this day." After Ferguson stares at Michael for a few moments he goes back to check his paperwork and does an inmate headcount for the first floor. At 8 am the inmates are allowed to go for their breakfast and the jail cells are automatically opened so that inmates can walk down to the cafeteria area. Michael is still sleeping as his jail cell opens and he doesn't really know where to go as Ferguson yells instructions at the inmates. Michael looks through the bars into the area where the corrections officers sit and asks Ferguson a question.

"Sir where do I go?" asks Michael. "Is it straight ahead."

"Just follow everybody else rapist," says Ferguson, Niggers like you shouldn't even be allowed to sleep."

"I ain't no nigger white boy," says Michael angrily, you better watch your mouth." An inmate walking to the cafeteria with Michael talks to him.

"Hey man leave Ferguson alone," says the inmate to Michael, he is just looking for an excuse to kick your head in. He will call several of those dirty officers and they will beat the hell out of you and nothing will be done about it."

"You better talk to him Mendoza," says Ferguson, tell him how things are run around here, we don't like rapists in this jail and somebody probably needs to teach him a lesson about how to treat women." Michael just walks straight ahead as several officers watch the inmates as they go to the first-floor lunch area. Michael walks into the large cafeteria and sees Carlton from the seventh-floor pod.

"You down here now?" asks Michael. "That was quick."

"I told you they were making me trustee, " says Carlton as he sweeps the floor and cleans, " this is my area." Michael looks at the food being served and it looks like garbage and he watches the Officers working the cafeteria as they talk to the inmates very rudely and push around the older inmates and treat them like animals. Michael goes through the line and gets his food and goes and sits down.

"They treat these people like animals,' whispers Michael.

"Yea," says an older black man named Raymond, as Michael sits down to try to consume his "slop," "modern day jails are privatized. Actors, B Ball players, politicians, they all own a piece of these jails. That's why they lock up so many people, they get dollars off our heads every night. And free labor, we go out every day and clean up the city and we plant and harvest food and ship it out. They make billions off us and the police herd us in here like cattle." As Raymond talks, Carlton approaches the table and as he does a large black inmate pushes him in the back and knocks him over and Michael naively jumps up from the table and pushes the large black inmate in the back in Carlton's defense. The inmate grabs Michael and throws him to the floor as the officers come over and break up the fight. One officer has a baton around Michael's neck and ushers him back to the cell.

"You know you're going to have a very unpleasant stay here if you keep doing shit like that," says the officer, you better ask some of the other guests how things go around here. No breakfast for your ass."

" I didn't want that nasty shit no way," whispers Michael.

"You say something," says the officer, meanly looking at Michael, I didn't think so." The officer has Ferguson open Michael's cell and he throws him in. As the officer leaves Ferguson approaches Michael's cell.

"I can't wait to beat your fucking head in," says Officer Ferguson, it's just a matter of time Alexander, just a matter of time." Ferguson walks back to his post. Michael is not really hurt, only a few bruises, a stiff neck, and a bruised ego. He just lays back down on his cot and tries to read one of the magazines in his cell.

CHAPTER 32

MAKING PLANS

As Michael sits in his cell of solitude, Officer Andrews and Corrections Officer Givhan are about 30 minutes into their breakfast.

"So why you want to have breakfast with me this morning Andrews," says Givhan, is it about Michael Alexander."

" Look brother I'm going to keep it straight," says Officer Andrews, have you ever heard of Coretta James."

"Of course, man," says Givhan, impressive black woman, ruthless they say but very rich, and really easy on the eyes."

"Yeah," says Officer Andrews, real ruthless. She's got a thing for Michael, a kind of weird obsession. Here's the question, how do you like your job."

"What," says Givhan, I hate that shit, you know. I hate looking at those prisoners every day with no hope, getting fucked in the ass and killed and I can go on and on. Why?"

" What would you do for 10 million dollars?" asks Officer Andrews."

"A lot," says Givhan, you know my situation." Officer Givhan is 35 years old from Compton and the only child of two 70 something-year-old parents that he provides care for.

"Michael and I became friends a few years ago and Coretta is adamant that there is no way he could have committed these crimes," says Officer Andrews, and to be honest with you, the Michael I know would never do this. We went to Jamaica together 5 or 6 years ago and took care of a rapist and then he turns around and does the same thing, it makes no sense."

"What do you mean took care of," asks Givhan.

"Exactly what you think I mean," says officer Andrews, this fucker Stephen Davis, he was the worst I've ever seen."

"Yeah, until your boy Michael," says Givhan, and what about all that evidence, DNA doesn't lie."

"I can't explain that," says Officer Andrews, but that's not him."

" Ok," says Givhan, so what you want me to do, I'll watch him for you as long as he is on the first floor but you know they only gonna keep him there so long."

"Help me break him out," says Officer Andrews, I will give you ten million dollars."

"How," says Givhan, there ain't no way we can get him out of there."

"Well we got to think of something and it's got to happen quickly before they move him or someone tries to kill him," says Officer Andrews, you know that racist ass Ferguson is capable of anything."

"Man if I do this shit they'll lock me up," says Givhan, Andrews you have lost your mind."

"Look," says Officer Andrews, you just have to get lost, and you will have ten million dollars to get lost with. Coretta James has all the assets you will need and a private jet that can fly you anywhere in the world and you can pay your parents' medical bills and make sure they are taken care of." Givhan gets up and leaves and drops a ten-dollar bill on the table and heads towards the door.

"Rodney," says Officer Andrews, just think about it okay."Givhan walks out fast and goes to his car and officer Andrews does not know where Givhan's head is. Andrews pays the check and heads out the door as Coretta James phone's him.

"You figured out how to get Michael out yet?" asks Coretta. "The clock is ticking." I didn't say I was gonna help you," says Officer Andrews slyly.

"You didn't say you wouldn't either, remember the hundred grand you took," says Correta. "Make something happen Detective."

"I'm working on it," says Officer Andrews, I'll call you when I know something." Officer Andrews thinks of other means to get Michael out as he gets in his car.

Meanwhile, it's 9:30 am at the jail and Michael has fallen asleep when he here's a slight tap on his cell from the new trustee Carlton.

"Hey man," says Carlton. "That was a real solid what you did for me. Nobody in this jail is crazy enough to stand up to Houston."

"I didn't stand up very long," says Michael. "He put me on my ass quickly."

"Man he is 6ft 4in,300lbs of muscle. He's beaten or killed a lot of inmates in this jail, he's not a good enemy to have and he's got a crew that follows him, even some of the officers fear him." "Here man," says Carlton as he hands Michael something wrapped in a dirty cloth, take this." Michael opens up the dirty cloth to see a man-made jailhouse knife.

"What's this?" asks Michael. "A knife."

"A shank," says Carlton. "You're gonna need this. I overheard some of the Officers talking after you left and they want to break you in quick to teach you a lesson and show you how things go around here. They hate rapists, one of the officers' sister was assaulted years ago and they take that shit personally."

"I told you I didn't rape nobody," says Michael.

"That shit doesn't matter," says Carlton. "Them motherfuckers don't care if you did it or not, they love degrading people around here as if being in this cell is not degrading enough. And Houston is the real rapist, he rapes men in here and the officers know it and they do nothing. That motherfucker got a 13-inch dick."

"How do you know his big his dick is?" asks Michael.

Carlton just holds his head down in shame and Michael gets the message.

"Look," says Carlton. "I don't know when but sometimes today they gonna call you out of this cell and they gonna put you and Houston someplace alone, you gotta kill that motherfucker."

"Carlton I don't want to kill nobody," says Michael.

"Man do want to get fucked in the ass?" asks Carlton.

"Definitely not," says Michael.

"You got two choices in here Michael," says Carlton. "Kill or be killed and it's up to you to choose which one you want." At that moment officer Ferguson yells at Carlton.

"Get away from that cell trustee, he yells, you won't be a trustee for long if you keep fraternizing with the prisoners like that."

"Yes sir," says Carlton as he walks away from Michael's enclosure. A few moments after Carlton leaves Michael's cell the door opens and Michael wonders what is going on. Ferguson looks into the hallway and points Michael towards the Chapel for the Sunday church service." After you finish with that bullshit service just walk back down here and I will open your cell and let you back in, "boy," says Ferguson, as the old saying goes, your soul belongs to God but your ass belongs to me." Michael doesn't even acknowledge the blasphemous talk and heads in the direction of the Chapel hoping not to run into Houston on the way. Michael enters the Chapel and Bishop Paul Smith, a 30 something-year-old Bishop conducts the service.

"Brothers let not your heart not be troubled by your incarceration," says Bishop Smith, for God can see your plight and knows the goodness of your heart. But it is in The Chapel of God and nowhere else can you be taught the true meaning of faith. The Bible is clear about God's love for the poor and disenfranchised people of the world. The Church has been charged with the responsibility of interpreting, preaching, and teaching of the word. It is on the basis of the word that the Church can invoke the words of 1 John to prove that the treatment of the poor and incarcerated people of the world is not God like when it says, If anyone has the world's goods and sees his brother in need yet closes his heart against him, how does God's love abide in him? Brothers, let us not love in word or speech but in deed and truth (John 3:17-18). So remember that God sees your plight and those who conspire against you and he will hold them accountable. Woe unto them that also use your incarceration for worldly gain. It is left up to us in the Church to stand up for you and fill in the gaps that the evil one has created. The Bible truly warns of such treatment of his people in Luke when he says," woe to you that are rich: woe to you that are full now: woe to you that laugh now: and blessed are you that hunger now: Blessed are you that weep now: blessed to you poor for yours is the kingdom of God.(Luke 6:20-26).The Church must stand up for those who cannot stand for themselves."

As the Bishop finishes up his sermon Michael asks if he can speak to him alone.

"Bishop Smith, he says , my name is Michael Alexander and I know you have heard this a million times but I am totally innocent of my crimes."

"I'm not here to judge you brother," says Bishop Smith, I have not lived a perfect life myself."

"Today I'm going to have to do something that I don't want to do but I have no other choice," says Michael. "And my heart is heavy."

"There's always a choice brother," says Bishop Smith, the question is are you strong enough to make the right one. Abraham was called upon by God to sacrifice his son Issac as a test of his faith and it was the hardest thing he ever had to do but his faith in God was true and he trusted God and God provided a lamb to sacrifice in place of his son. I pray God provides a way out for you. Be blessed good brother," says the Bishop as he leaves.

Michael is absolutely certain that he must kill Houston and he returns to his cell and looks for the shank that Carlton provided but finds it missing.

" You are looking for this," says Ferguson as he stands outside the cell, we randomly inspect the cells. I'm sure this isn't yours, the last inmate must have left it," says Ferguson with a smile on his face. Michael knows Ferguson is part of whatever is soon to happen to him and he knows that he cannot defeat Houston alone.

While Michael sits in his cell of worry, Officer Andrews sits at his desk wondering not only if Givhan will help him but also if he will" rat" him out and have him locked up. At about 11 am Officer Andrews receives a call from Givhan.

"Andrews, he says , I've been thinking, I can't pass up this opportunity and I think I know how we can do it when my shift ends tomorrow."

"Wait a minute," says Officer Andrews, don't say anything on the phone."

"Okay," says Givhan, I need some sleep but when I get up I will call you so when can meet up." With that he hangs up the phone and tries to get some well-deserved sleep.

CHAPTER 33

SACRIFICIAL LAMB

Back at the jail, Michael finds it hard to sleep and looks out of his cell and sees several of the officers huddled up together and he wonders what the conversation is about. He has been locked down all day except for the few moments he went out for breakfast and the time at the Chapel. At about 1 pm that afternoon, Michael is sitting in his cell when his cell door opens and Ferguson calls him to come to the front.

"Alexander," says Ferguson, it's shower time for you. The shower is free and you can take your time."

"I don't want no shower," says Michael. "Ain't no women in here for me to get cleaned up for."

"Well," says Ferguson, I'm sure you can find yourself a girlfriend if you want to."

"I don't," says Michael. "I would prefer to remain in the cell." Michael knows that the time has come for him to face Houston and he knows it will be in the shower. Ferguson points Michael to the shower and demands that he go and tells him there will be towels waiting for him. Michael heads to his potential of death determined to walk away from the incident not only alive but also having not been raped. Michael walks into the shower and hears the shower running and his fear and anxiety go up several notches. He notices that although there are several Officers that work the floor strangely none of them are on the floor at the time, only a few trustees are on the floor. Michael looks up and stepping out of the shower is the giant Houston with his hand on his crotch. Michael is terrified but tries to show no fear as the monstrous-looking Houston stares at him.

"I'm going to teach you a lesson you will never forget," says Houston, then you gonna be my bitch."

"Never in this lifetime," says Michael. "You gotta kill me to fuck me." As Michael stares at Houston who starts to take off his clothes neither man realizes that eyes are on them. Houston undresses and looks at Michael and starts to move towards him when someone rushes him from behind and as Houston turns around the person stabs him in the neck and Houston falls to the floor in pain grabbing his neck, bleeding very badly gasping for breath and after a few moments, the monster they called Houston is dead. Michael stands there in a stunned daze looking at Houston's dead body.

"Help me pull him in the shower," says the voice, throw this down that drain."

"Carlton what the fuck man," says Michael. "He's dead." Michael helps Carlton carry Houston's body into the running shower.

"Look says Michael. "Put the shank in his hand and lay his arm on his chest and they'll think he killed himself. Let the shank just fall to the floor as if he just dropped it. Leave the shower running so most of the blood will run down the drain"

"Yeah, good thinking," says a nervous Carlton. Here give me those clothes and put this jumpsuit on and hurry and get in the other shower and wash that blood off. I saw Ferguson take that shank from your cell with his racist ass, I wasn't gonna let Houston do to you what he did to me. Get out of here man and dry off and give me your bloody shit so I can get rid of it." Michael hurries and changes his clothes and Carlton takes all the clothes and tosses them away.

"Go back to your cell and act like nothing happened," says Carlton. "The Officers won't be back right away because they set this up and they have to give Houston enough time to assault you, I think he was supposed to kill you too."

"Why did do this for me Carlton?" asks Michael. "You risked everything for me."

"You did the same thing for me this morning in that cafeteria," says Carlton. "I'm a piece of shit, I wasn't a piece of shit when I came in here but I'm a piece of shit now. I believe you when you say you're innocent and you can't prove your innocence if you're dead." Michael walks back down towards his cell and Ferguson has stepped away thankfully and the Corrections officer on duty opens Michael's cell and allows him to go in and he simply lays down as if nothing has happened, nervous as hell but staying cool. He remembers the words of Bishop Smith and believes that a lamb has been provided for him. Carlton discards all the bloody clothes for Michael and himself and pretends to be sweeping floors and going about his trustee business. After about 15 minutes Ferguson returns to his post and the other officers also return as if they were together all the time. Carlton continues to do his work and goes into the kitchen to help with kitchen duties when a trustee comes out of the bathroom and yells for the officers. The crooked Officers run down expecting to see Michael in the shower but instead they find a nude Houston lying dead in the running shower drenched and most of the blood from the crime scene has went down the shower drain. Houston has the knife near his hand as if he possibly has killed himself. The officers call the jailhouse morgue and Ferguson rushes to Michael's cell as he pretends to be sleep. "Alexander wake up," says Ferguson, what happened in that shower."

"What do you mean?" asks Michael sheepishly. "I showered and came out."

"You were in there by yourself, asks Ferguson, you didn't see anything."

"No," says Michael. "You told me I would be alone and I was alone. Thank you for that cause I don't like showering with a lot of guys." Ferguson doesn't believe Michael but tries to play coy because he was a big part of setting up Michael and he did tell Michael he would be alone in the shower.

"And you didn't see anything at all, asks Ferguson, nothing unusual."

"Nothing," says Michael. "I'm glad you made me take a shower, I needed that." Ferguson leaves and meets the people and other detectives investigating the murder. Michael is scared but says nothing. Later that afternoon he watches as Houston's body rolls past his cell headed to the morgue.

Later that evening Officer Givhan wakes up from his slumber and calls Officer Andrews who answers.

"Man you've been sleeping all day," says Officer Andrews, more like hibernating."

"Man that night shift kicked my ass," says Givhan, look, I want to meet with Coretta James before I go to work so set it up. I think I know how to get him out of there but after that I gotta get lost."

"I'll set it up," says Andrews. "Be ready to roll." Officer Andrews calls Coretta James who insists that they meet immediately and suggests an abandoned chicken plant in Van Nuys and they all head for the location.

Back in LA County jail Michael is called from his cell and asked to meet with a Lieutenant Turner who is investigating the death of inmate Houston. Turner is a 5 ft 11in black man and a 20 year veteran and Michael sits in the office.

"Mr. Alexander," says the Officer, I'm Lieutenant Dan Turner, and I just want to ask you a few questions, now did you see Marcus Houston anywhere in the shower area."

"No," says Michael. "I took a quick shower and came back and no one was there but me. I did think it was unusual that Ferguson forced me to take a shower."

"What do you mean forced, asks Lieutenant Turner, he told you had to shower."

"Hell yea," says Michael. "And there were no Officers anywhere around, looks like he was setting me up for something. I think they use Houston around here like they used black men back in slavery, they would have black men rape other black men openly in front of everyone and take away their manhood, embarrass them and hopefully take away their desire for physical freedom. I think they tried to set me up like that but thank God it didn't work out that way. And just for the record I would die for my manhood. The world has taken everything from black men and our dignity is all we have left, I will die for mine."

"Did you kill him Alexander, asks Lieutenant Turner, and if you didn't do you know who did." "No and no," says Michael. "And even if I did I wouldn't tell you." Lieutenant Turner is impressed with Michael and though he doesn't necessarily believe him he respects his convictions. Turner waves to Officer Ferguson to open up Michael's cell.

"You're free to go Mr. Alexander," says Lieutenant Turner, good luck.

Michael looks back at Lieutenant Turner and points at Officer Ferguson.

"Y'all better keep an eye on that racist ass white man," says Michael. "He doesn't respect the law of God or the law of man."

Michael exits the room and goes through the gate and back to his cell where the trustees have brought his lunch to the cell to keep him out of the general population. Inside the cell he finds a note from Carlton that says

"They 're gonna move you tomorrow," says the note, the Officers feel humiliated by you and they want some get back."

Michael just tries to eat lunch and go to sleep.

Back in Van Nuys, Coretta's Limo, Givhans red Camaro and Officer Andrews in his unmarked police car pull up to the abandoned plant and the three of them get out and after Coretta is introduced to Givhan he tells them his plan.

"Look, the only way I see we get Mr. Alexander out of there is to walk him right out the front door," says Givhan, and keep it moving from there."

"Out the front door, yells Officer Andrews, how?" "Look," says Givhan, that racist ass Ferguson is 6 ft 4 and Mr. Alexander is about the same, maybe a little taller, so we walk him out in Ferguson's uniform."

"And where Ferguson gonna be, ask Officer Andrews, he's just gonna give Michael his clothes."

"Come on man you know he's not gonna do that," says Givhan," we're gonna undress his white ass. Ms. James, I'm gonna need to get out of the country, somewhere with no extradition with the U.S. and where I can spend that money Andrews promised me in peace. Oh, I'm also going to need my parents taken care.

""My pilot will fly you out as soon as you leave that jail," says Correta. "Your parents will be taken care of, don't worry."

"Andrews, I'm going to need you there in the morning when I get off," says Givhan, you're gonna help me take that white racist down, I'm actually looking forward to this.

"With that the three of them go their separate ways and Givhan has to not only get ready to go to work but he has eight hours of work to ready himself to possibly release Michael and for his life to change forever.

That night Givhan goes to the East Bay home for the elderly and says a solemn and sorrowful goodbye to his mother and father who both suffer from Dementia and Givhan is not sure if his parents understand what he is saying but he tells them both goodbye. Back at LA County jail Michael has a visitor and is taken to the visitation room where he sees Officer Andrews for the first time in quite a while.

"Dana Andrews," says Michael. "To what do I owe the pleasure of this visit."

"Wanted to check on you boy," says Officer Andrews," you know running around with you cost me my stripes, no more Detective. Be ready in the morning because we're going to make a move, rest up tonight and be ready to go. That's all I can tell you here. Had to give you some hope brother, hope is a good thing."

"One of the best things," says Michael," thanks man for giving me something to look forward to." Officer Andrews leaves and Michael goes back to his cell where Ferguson is waiting for him and he grabs Michael and takes him to the hole or solitary confinement and Michael is thrown in where it is cold and dark and he is really concerned about what may happen to him that night.

CHAPTER 34

THE GREAT ESCAPE

At about 10:30 pm Officer Givhan arrives early for his 11pm shift and gets ready to make his count as Ferguson heads towards the front to finish up the rest of his shift. Givhan looks across into Michael's cell and notices he is gone.

"Where's Mr. Alexander, asks Officer Givhan worrying about his plans, was he moved?"

"Yeah," says Ferguson, I moved his ass to solitary, the solitary hole. You know that prisoner Marcus Houston was found dead tonight and I believe Michael Alexander was involved. I figured a night or two in the hole might refresh his memory."

"You mean your Buck buster Houston is dead," says Givhan, couldn't happen to a nicer guy."

"Buck buster," says Ferguson, you know Givhan you're a pussy, soft, that's why these inmates run over your ass. You have to put them in their place to get their respect."

"Keep the niggers and the Mexicans in their place," says Givhan, is that what you mean Ferguson." "You said it, I didn't," says Ferguson, have a good night, I'll see you in the morning." Ferguson leaves and Givhan rushes to get Michael out of solitary confinement and he pulls a shaken Michael out of the cold and damp solitary hole.

"Scary in there huh, ask Givhan, you ok."

"I'll live," says Michael," that dirty ass Ferguson put me in there. I believe he tried to get me killed earlier."

"How did you get out of that shit, asks Givhan, that sick ass Houston gets a lot of pleasure out of dehumanizing his fellow inmates."

"I had a guardian Angel," says Michael. "Literally." Givhan walks Michael back to the cell and talks to him.

"I'm working with Andrews," says Givhan, Coretta James and Andrews and myself are working to get you out of here in the morning. Be ready, when it's time to move we gotta move."

"I'll be ready for whatever," says Michael. "Don't worry."

"I'm not worried," says Givhan, Coretta James really got your back. I'll get the trustees to bring you some food. Sleep well brother." Givhan goes about his normal duties while preparing for the morning. He goes into his bag and grabs some CHC13 or chloroform and several other tools of the trade and readies his mind. The next morning at 6am Officer Andrews pulls up to the front of the LA County jail and heads towards the door to go inside the building.

"Andrews," says the officer on duty, you know you have to take off your gun. You can't have that around the inmates." Officer Andrews takes off his gun and leaves it at the desk and goes to the part of the jail where Michael is being held and sees Givhan readying himself.

"What's the plan Givhan," says Officer Andrews, how are we gonna do this?"

"Ferguson always comes in early," says Givhan, and his routine is the same. He gonna say something smart and then he gonna go in there to change. I'm going to follow him and we got to grab his big ass and knock him out, one way or another. I got this chloroform but it takes time, we gotta get him off his feet and undress his no good ass."

"Okay," says Andrews. " I'm ready to go." Givhan goes back to the front and waits and Michael is awake in his cell and looks across the bay at Givhan. At 6:30 am Ferguson comes walking through the door for his 7am shift.

"If it isn't Pussy ass Givhan," says Ferguson, you can go now and let a man take over."

"Where is that man at," says Givhan, I don't know what you are." Ferguson goes in the back to put down his bag and Givhan follows and as soon as Ferguson enters the room Andrews hits him in the back of the head and he falls to the floor. Givhan looks at Officer Andrews.

"Sometimes that chloroform don't work and we don't have time to mess around," says Officer Andrews, come on let's take off this uniform." Andrews and Givhan take off Fergusons uniform and they see a tattooed man with racial tats' all over his body. After removing his uniform they tape his mouth and hands and Givhan goes to Michael's cell with the uniform.

"Mr. Alexander put this on," says Givhan, hurry up." Michael takes off the prison jumpsuit and puts on Ferguson's uniform which is slightly short but fits relatively well. Next Givhan and Michael go back across the hall in the guard room and put the prison jumpsuit on Ferguson who is starting to wake. Ferguson starts to groan and looks over at Michael with his uniform.

"Ferguson," says Givhan, I've been waiting a long time to do this."Givhan bitch slaps Ferguson.

"We don't have time for that," says Andrews. " Where we gonna take him."

"Come on," says Givhan, I got an idea." The two men drag Ferguson to the yard with his mouth and hands duck taped and leave him there and Givhan goes back and opens up the first floor cells and allows the inmates to go to the yard.

"I'll take Michael," says Detective Andrews, "Coretta is parked on the side and she's going to get you to her plane. Good luck brother and thanks." Michael follows Officer Andrews around the corridor and out the front all while wearing Ferguson's uniform and walks out of the front door and the two men start out the building. "Andrews, yells the attending Officer, don't forget your gun." Officer Andrews retrieves his gun and the two men hurry out the building and jump into Officer Andrews' car as Givhan goes around where Coretta is waiting and her car takes off. Back inside the jail on the first floor the inmates hit the yard and they notice an inmate walking groggy across the yard with his mouth taped up. One inmate removes the tape and can't believe that Officer Ferguson is the person in the inmate uniform. The inmate starts to smile.

"Look at this shit," says the inmate, it's that bitch Ferguson."
All the inmates gather around Ferguson and start to chant and
they start to mercilessly beat and kick Ferguson.

Back in Coretta's rented Toyota she passes 10 million
dollars to Givhan and expresses her extreme gratitude.

"I don't know how you pulled this off," says Correta.
"But you got Michael out and that's all that matters. I have
a beautiful compound in Morocco and they will never find
you and even if they did they do they couldn't send you back.
Beautiful land full of beautiful ladies, paradise." Coretta takes
Givhan directly to her awaiting plane and Givhan gets on the
plane and it takes off for Morocco and he immediately pours
himself a drink and relaxes and has a big sigh of relief.

Inside of Officer Andrews' car, Michael exhales for a
moment not believing that he is out in the public again.

"Man did you put that shit together?" asks Michael. "I
can't believe I'm out."

'Givhan put that together," says Officer Andrews, Givhan
knew that Ferguson was a creature of habit and he used it
against him."

"Ferguson was a dirty man," says Michael. "His racist ass just didn't care at all. What do you think the inmates will do to him in the yard."

"They hated his ass with a passion," says Officer Andrews, he treated those inmates like animals. There is no way he leaves that yard alive, no way. I can only imagine what they are doing to him."

CHAPTER 35

THE PSYCHIC

As Officer Andrews speaks the phone rings and Captain Richardson, Andrews supervisor, is on the phone with Officer Andrews not knowing what to expect.

"What's up Cap," says Officer Andrews, what's going on."

"I got a job for you," says the Captain, I know you've been trying to get your stripes back and I need your help on a case and this will go a long way towards that goal."

"What do you need me to do Cap, asks Officer Andrews, you know I'm at your service."

"You know that young girl that disappeared the other day from Beverly Hills, her name is Karyn Rodman, asks the Captain, well we are desperate to find her. Her family is riding our back and so is the papers and the general public and we are trying any and everything so a psychic called and volunteered her services and we need you to pick her up and take her over there. Sanchez is unavailable and I need you."

"You can count on me Cap," says Officer Andrews, what do I do."

"Just pick her up and take her to the mother's house," says the Captain, just let her do whatever she does. I will text you her address, her name is Pat Bailey. She is expecting you." The Captain hangs up and Michael is upset.

"Man we got to get off these streets," says Michael. "Somebody might spot me."

"You're in a police car," says Andrews. "And besides I want to help find this girl. Her family is Black and she went over to her boyfriend's house the other night and never came back home. She is a straight A student and runs track and plays in the band, I got to help. I'll get you home right after." As officer Andrews heads to pick up the psychic the Officers at LA County jail notices the inmates on the first floor have not made it to breakfast and are hanging around outside in the yard. Several officers go to the floor to check and they walk outside and see something laying outside in the yard and they rang the alarm and all the inmates are ushered back inside. The officers look at the clothes and they realize that there is a dead man in the yard but he is so badly beaten he is unrecognizable.

"Wow ,says one Officer, I have never seen anyone beaten this bad. I have no idea who this inmate is. Go check and see where Michael Alexander is." An officer goes to Check on Michael Alexander's cell and then he checks the hole and they are both empty. An Officer recognizes the Corpse based on Ferguson's name on a wrist band he wears.

"This is Ferguson," says one Officer, I recognize his arm band and some of those tattoos, they messed him up bad." The Officer looking for Michael returns.

"Alexander is gone," says the Officer, he is not in his cell and not in the hole and was not moved off the floor, I don't know where he is." The Officers wait for help and they leave Ferguson's body where they found it for forensics.

Back in Officer Andrews car they pick up the psychic Pat Bailey and head towards the missing girl's house.

"Ms. Bailey," says Officer Andrews, I am Officer Andrews and that's my partner in the back Officer Alex." Ms. Bailey, an attractive white woman looks in the back at Michael.

"You have had a few rough days lately haven't you sir," says the psychic, are you going to run for the rest of your life."

"Excuse me," says Michael. "What do you mean?" "Your aura hangs all over this car," says the psychic, you still have a tough road ahead." Michael doesn't say anything else to the psychic and just continues to ride in the back seat. Michael and Officer are both well aware of what they just went through and hope that what they are experiencing now won't jeopardize their ill gotten freedom. The psychic is very interested in Michael.

"Michael," says the psychic, let me hold your hand."

"What," says Michael. "We can't get it on in the car." "Don't worry," says the psychic, I won't be one of your Gigolo conquests. How is your daughter these days?" Michael wonders how the psychic knows so much about him.

"You're deep into that Voo Doo shit," says Michael to the psychic, who told you about my daughter?" "No Voo Doo Michael," says the psychic, my gift comes from God, I have always been able to see things, that's how I know about your daughter, I can see her."

"God," says Michael. "People don't believe in God no more."

"I do Michael," says the psychic, and you do too. How do you think you always find a way out of no way. It takes a lot of faith to believe in something you can't physically see." Michael and the psychic continue their intriguing conversations as Officer Andrews pulls up to the address of Karyn Rodman's mothers house. The psychic Pat Bailey exits first and Officers Andrews gives Michael instructions.

"Of course I don't have to tell you to stay in the car and stay down," says Officer Andrews, we'll be back,"

"How long?" asks Michael. "I can't be hanging around on these streets."

"Don't worry about that just stay down," says Officer Andrews. The Rodman family lives in a 5000 sq ft house on the end of Rodeo Dr. on the outskirts of Beverly Hills. The house is considered modest for the area but very nice and the family is moderately wealthy. Karyn lived in the house with her mother Gail and her little brother Tim, Gail and her husband Robert are going through a divorce. Detective Andrews rings the doorbell and Gail Rodman answers.

"Hello , can I help you?," says Gail. Officer Andrews pulls out his badge and shows it to the woman.

"I'm Officer Dana Andrews and this is my assistant Pat Bailey," says Officer Andrews, and we are investigating your daughter Karyn's disappearance, may we come in and ask you a few more questions." Officer Andrews notices the news on with a report of Michael's escape. He doesn't introduce Pat Bailey as a psychic as not to alarm the mother. Gail Rodman is somewhat rude to the woman and Officer Andrews.

"I already told you police everything I know," says Gail, if you weren't wasting your time over here with me and you were out looking for Karyn maybe we could find her." The psychic feels uncomfortable with Gail Rodman's attitude.

"Ma'am," says the psychic, do you mind if I take a look into your daughter's room. It might give me an idea of who your daughter was." Gail Rodman reluctantly agrees and leads Pat Bailey down the hall to her daughter's room. Karyn has a large bedroom with typical teenage stuff laying around next to her computer and desk and her nice queen sized bed. The psychic Pat Bailey looks around the girl's room and stares up at the roof and gently lays down across the girls bed under the watchful eye of Gail Rodman. After a few moments of laying on the bed the psychic sits straight up and turns her head to the left and the missing teenager Karyn Parsons starts to speak through her. Her eyes bulge out and she looks directly at Gail Rodman and says,

"Mommy please tell them where you buried me." Gail Rodman begins to scream loudly and Officer Andrews races towards the room.

"Get out here, yells Gail, get out of here ,you're a witch, get out of here." Gail pushes Officer Andrews and the psychic Pat Bailey out of her house and officer Andrews returns to the car and asks Pat Bailey what happened in there.

"She killed her daughter and buried her somewhere, say Pat Bailey, she did it herself." "How did you figure that out, asks Officer Andrews as a stunned Michael looks on, did she tell you."

"No," says the psychic, Karyn told me." Detective Andrews looks back at Michael and calls his Captain.

"Captain Richardson," says Officer Andrews, I think you need to send a car back over to the Rodman residence," says Officer Andrews, I think Mrs. Rodman is responsible for killing her own daughter."

"Really," says Captain Richardson, that's unbelievable, I'll get a team right out there. You're not going to believe this Andrews but Michael Alexander escaped from LA County."

"Really," says Officer Andrews while looking in the rear view mirror at Michael, how did that happen." "They think one of the corrections Officers helped him," says Captain Richardson, and get this, one of the Corrections was beaten to death by some of the inmates. And it looks like Alexander just walked right out of the building dressed as Ferguson. Anyway, good job Andrews." They hang up and the psychic just looks at Officer Andrews and says, "what a tangled web we weave." As the car nears the psychic's home Michael is extremely anxious and wants to get off the streets and as soon as the car stops he jumps out and the psychic gets out, Michael makes an observation.

"Fine woman," says Michael. "Too bad she is so strange." Michael exits the back seat and the psychic again asks if she can hold his right hand and he again declines.

"What are you afraid of Michael," says the Psychic, if I'm as strange as you think I am then what do you have to lose." Michael feels the psychic is reading his mind and extends his right hand. The psychic cradles Michael's hand into her own right hand and immediately drops Michael hand and steps back.

"You have two right hands Michael," says the psychic, and one of them has blood on it ,a lot of blood. There's a devil chasing you Michael, a devil that knows you better than you know yourself and he's out for revenge."

"A devil," says Michael. "Revenge, revenge for what."

"Always know where you are Michael," says the psychic, there's a secret, a secret that will soon be revealed." With that the psychic walks off leaving Michael and Officer Andrews shaken. Officer Andrews revs up the car and he and Michael head towards Coretta's Hollywood Hills estate where everyone anxiously await their arrival. Michael talks to Officer Andrews.

"That's a weird white woman but she sure is fine," says Michael. "She's deep."

"How can you be talking about ass at a time like this," says Officer Andrews, did you listen to the stuff she said."

"Yeah," says Michael. "That stuff is way out there. And to answer your other question, I just left a jail full of men, that's how I can think about ass at a time like this. But, I do wonder what that psychic meant about me having two right hands and one having blood on it."

"That is weird," says Officer Andrews, I have never heard anything like that before. She knows something though."

"Maybe I'll go back over there one day and ask her fine ass what she knows," says Michael. "Get to the bottom of it if you know what I mean."

"Man you crazy," says the Officer, with your hoeish ass, you'll be laid up with another woman and that psychic will magically appear in your bedroom and start talking to you."

"Yea," says Michael. "That's some scary shit."

CHAPTER 36

THE DEVIL IN NEW ORLEANS

The two men conversate and finally make their way to Coretta's Hollywood Hills hideout. Although the hideaway is off the radar Coretta has several of her men keeping a close eye on the comings and goings towards her abode. Michael sees the villa as a sight for sore eyes and immediately runs towards the door where Cheryl runs and jumps in his arms wearing new clothes brought to the house by Coretta and Donald is also standing close by with a broad grin on his face very happy to see Michael, happy to see his "brother " Mike.

"Hi Michael ,says Cheryl gushing, I am so happy to see you." Cheryl has tight grip around Michael's neck and Officer Andrews is puzzled knowing that Cheryl was once married to Kenneth who was at one time Michael's best friend. Coretta stands close by waiting for Cheryl to release Michael so she can embrace him. Cheryl finally loosens her grip on Michael and Coretta comes over and kisses Michael and embraces him and is genuinely excited to see him.

"I am so happy to see you Michael," says Correta. "How are you, did they hurt you in there."

"They tried," says Michael. "But I'm here in one piece." Coretta walks away from Michael and gives Officer Andrews a very large bag and thanks him for what he did.

"What's in that bag," says Michael. "Now I see why you're breaking your neck for me, I thought you had my back."

"I do have your back," says Officer Andrews, do you know what I risked to try to get you out of there?"

"Yeah," says Michael. "You did risk a lot but the reward seems to be pretty sweet also. You can't even carry that heavy bag."

"I have been keeping up with it on TV," says Donald, that racist Officer was killed by the inmates and they are trying to find that Officer Givhan."

"Good luck with that," says Coretta," he's long gone."

"Dirty ass Ferguson," says Michael. "It couldn't have happened to a nicer guy."

"What about you Officer Andrews?" asks Coretta. "You think they are gonna figure out you are involved? All that money won't do you any good if you're locked up. Oh, and may I see your cell phone please?"

"Why, asks Officer Andrews, don't you have your own phone." Coretta just extends her hand and motions for the phone and Officer Andrews reluctantly hands it over. Coretta drops the phone on the ground and stomps it and then throws it into the fireplace.

"In case they do figure you out this is an automatic tracking device," says Correta. "We don't need unwanted company. Get something that can't be traced."

"I paid a thousand dollars for that phone," says Officer Andrews, wow."

"You have millions in that bag," says Correta. "Also you may want to stay here off the radar for a while till we figure out what's going on. You may as well bunk in here with the rest of us." Officer Andrews never considered the price he may have to pay to free Michael and like everyone else he still wonders how Michael's DNA has been found at all the crime scenes. Coretta calls one of her employees over.

"Teddy," says Correta. "Get rid of that ugly ass police car." Teddy takes the keys from Officer Andrews and drives the car away from the area because Coretta believes that the Officer's car also may be able to be tracked.

Meanwhile, in Harrah's Casino in New Orleans a woman meets her escort for the night, he has flown all the way from Southern California. The woman is the very wealthy Tina Miller, a steel mogul and daughter of Author James Miller who is in town on business and she is ready to play. Ms. Miller's date meets her in the Casino lobby at the blackjack table. Ms. Miller is a mixed race black women, her father being white and mother a southern black woman from Atlanta. Ms. Miller greets her date a very tall dark complexioned black man with curly hair.

"Hello handsome," says Ms. Miller, I guess my ship sailed in tonight. What's your name again honey?"

"Michael," says the man, Michael Alexander."

"You come very highly recommended," says Ms. Miller, Coretta James said you are her best she has ever had."

"Well I aim to please," says her escort, let's enjoy a few hands of black jack and have a few drinks." The two of them sit down at the Black Jack table and order a few drinks and Ms. Miller thinks her escort is the perfect gentleman. He pulls her chair for her and caresses her back and is very attentive to her needs.

"Michael you are gorgeous," says Ms. Miller, where have you been all my life."

"I've been waiting for you all my life," says her escort," it was just a matter of time before we met." Ms. Miller and her escort continue to drink and gamble and have appetizers and after about 90 minutes Tina Miller is ready for a little more personal touch.

"I have a suite right next door at the Hilton," says Ms. Miller, I've got an itch that needs scratching."

"That's my specialty," says her escort, Michael Alexander aims to please." Tina Miller and her escort head next door to the Hilton and they take the elevator up to the top floor where there is a suite reserved for only their most privileged guests. Ms. Miller walks her guest into the suite and asks him to pour them a couple of glasses of champagne.

"Make yourself at home Michael," says Tina Miller, I'm going to take off this dress." Ms. Miller has on a beautiful yellow fitted dress and goes into the bathroom and comes out in a see through gown that showcases her very curvy body.

"Thought I would get into something relaxing," says Ms. Miller, just to let you know what I'm working." The escort takes another sip of champagne and grabs Tina and spins her around and rips off her gown forcefully.

"What are you doing Michael, asks Tina Miller, why are you so rough. I like things slow and easy, that's what I'm paying for."

"You'll take it any way I give it to you," says the escort, you know you like what I'm doing." At that moment he grabs Tina by her long hair and spins her around and slaps her and then he throws her down on the floor and he bites Ms. Miller across her right breast like an animal. He takes out his Penis and tries to force Ms. Millers head up but she fights him as he almost pulls her hair out. He tries to cover her mouth but Tina Miller moves his hand trying to block her mouth and screams loudly and the escort becomes rattled and jumps up off the floor and runs out of the hotel room and down the stairs and an older white man comes out of his room at the end of the hall and tries to stop the man as he heads for the exit but the escort simply runs over him and keeps going. Tina Miller struggles to her feet and dials 0 to get an operator and speaks as soon as the operator answers. As the operator answers she notices a man running full speed out of the lobby and out of the hotel.

"Front desk," answers the attendant.

"A man just assaulted me," says the voice on the other line, I need the police."

"Yes Ms. Miller," says the attendant, I will send up hotel security and I will also call the police." The attendant summons hotel security and calls the New Orleans Police to report the assault. The top floor of the Hilton in the French Quarter of New Orleans becomes a crime scene. At that time in Hollywood Hills, Michael is excited about getting his first night sleep away from the jail. All the bedrooms are filled in the house and Michael sits in one of the bedrooms and talks to Officer Andrews about the events of the day. Michael has showered and has on some pajamas and he is exhausted. The room has a queen sized bed and a small sofa and Michael is about to call it a night.

"What a day," says Michael. "This day could have turned out a lot different than it did and I feel really blessed to make it through. What's your next move Andrews?"

"I don't know," says Officer Andrews, I'm just going to sleep on it. I guess I got to stay in here, all the rooms are full."

"Yeah I guess," says Michael. "Good night brother." Michael lays down in the bed and notices Officer Andrews headed for the bed.

"Where you going man," says Michael. "I know you don't think you are getting in the bed with me."

"Why not," says Officer, I'm not gay."

"I don't care if you're gay or not," says Michael. "I'm not sleeping with no man, you better lay on that floor or across that love seat."

"You said you slept with your cousins when you were growing up," says Officer Andrews, didn't know you were homophobic."

"I didn't have a choice, we were poor and I don't have a phobia," says Michael. "But I don't sleep with men. And besides that I saw you with your shoes off."

"With my shoes off," says Officer Andrews.

"Yeah," says Michael. "I saw those long black Tony the Tiger Jurassic Park toenails, you accidentally touch me with them I'll need surgery, hell no, you choose, the love seat or the floor." With that Michael stops talking and tries to sleep and he will need his rest because he will receive more bad news tomorrow.

A couple of hours later Donald wakes up and is walking through the living room area and turns on the Television and CNN is broadcasting from New Orleans about the attempted rape of an Heiress. The report shows the Hilton Hotel and shows the perpetrator entering the hotel with Ms. Miller and running from the hotel full speed after the incident. Donald looks at the photo and the name across the bottom of the screen, Michael Alexander. Donald runs in the room where Michael is sleeping and sees Officer Andrews laying across the floor and Michael in the bed in a deep sleep. Donald awakens Officer Andrews on the floor. "Hey man ,says Donald, there's something on TV you have to see." The groggy Officer goes into the living room area and watches the live TV feed from New Orleans as a reporter speaks from the scene.

"DNA collected from the bite on the victim," says the reporter, matches that of alleged Southern California rapist Michael Alexander. Mr. Alexander was seen on video entering the hotel with Ms. Miller, he was also seen on video at Harrah's Casino next door dining and gambling with the victim and was later seen running away from the scene. Ms. Miller is shaken but she will survive the incident and just announced, the victim's father multi Billionaire Author James Miller has just offered a 10 million dollar reward for the arrest and conviction of Michael Alexander. Mr. Miller said he is willing to pay anyone who can even locate the "animal" as he refers to Mr. Alexander. This is Susan Davis reporting live from New Orleans back to you Phil." Donald and Officer Andrews just stare at each other because there is no way Michael could have been in two places at once yet the video clearly shows him at the scenes and his DNA is again at the scene of the crime.

"How do they get that DNA so fast?" asks Donald. "It only happened a few hours ago."

"Well they have this system called CODIS which means Combined DNA Index System which the FBI uses and they upload your DNA into the system once and every time you do something else and they put of a copy of your DNA in again it gets an instant hit," says Officer Andrews, they have millions of copies of DNA in the system. Every felon must give a DNA sample. This woman's father is wealthy so they rushed her DNA to the FBI."

"Man what we gonna do," says Donald, Michael is getting in deeper every day."

"Well let him sleep for now," says Officer Andrews, he's had a rough couple of days." As Donald and Officer Andrews talk the beautiful Cheryl comes into the living room area unable to sleep with a short pajama set on that doesn't leave much to the imagination.

"You gentleman in here developing a nice little bromance, jokes Cheryl, what's going on." Donald can't take his eyes off that short set.

"Damn girl," says Donald, have you been this fine all your life because you are wearing them shorts." Cheryl starts to respond but she sees the CNN report and stops in her tracks.

"Oh my God, asks Cheryl, how is this possible?" "It's possible," says Correta. "Coming into the room wearing tight black sleeping attire, and now I'm involved. According to my sources she is saying that I connected her with Michael. They're looking for me too now." Donald stands by staring at Coretta and Cheryl as everyone else in the room tries to figure out how and what is going on. Donald understands that they are in trouble but he cannot understand why officer Andrews hasn't even looked at Coretta or Cheryl, especially the way they are dressed. Donald pulls the Officer to the side.

"Hey man," says Donald, it's not my business but do you like women at all. I haven't seen you look at either one of those two fine creatures at all, what's your story?"

"What kind of question is that, asks Officer Andrews, man I love women. Unlike you brother, I had to develop the art of looking without looking. I'm a police Officer and I must appear to be non biased at all times and therefore I must appear to ignore all enticements. But just between you and me, Coretta James looks delicious."

"Cheryl ain't no slouch either," says Donald, body for days."

"No she's not," says Officer Andrews, but Cheryl is the bring home to mama type while Coretta is the type you take to Montego Bay and don't come out of the room the whole weekend." Donald looks at Officer Andrews a little differently and learns not to judge people by his prejudices.

"And besides brother Donald," says Officer Andrews, we got a lot to figure out with this shit, there's a lot going on and we are all in real deep." "Word up," says Donald, this shit ain't nothing to play with."

CHAPTER 37

A KILLER IS REVEALED

Back in New Orleans a man and a woman sit in a dark location and talk.

"This vendetta of yours is going to get us fucked up Marvin," says the woman, we need to lay low for a while and let things blow over a little bit."

"I ain't letting shit blow over," says the man named Marvin, I don't know how he got of that jail but he can't hide forever. Until they catch him, we stick with the plan. That bitch Michael Alexander is going down."

Back at the SOPD Lieutenant Towns and Sergeant Hall work the phones trying to find the whereabouts of Michael Alexander and still not putting together the connection between Michael Alexander and Officer Andrews and their connection with Coretta James. Frustration abounds all over the precinct as the Detectives try to figure out how Michael escaped.

"That Corrections Officer Givhan had to have some help," says Sergeant Hall, there's no way he could overpower Ferguson by himself. Have someone check to see the comings and goings around that time at the jail. Also, check the trustees, one of them may have helped him. We gotta get this murderer Michael Alexander."

"I just got word that our boy Michael just raped a billionaire's daughter in New Orleans," says Lieutenant Towns. "The woman's father just posted a 10 million dollar reward for Michael Alexander so believe me someone's going to give him up, it's just a matter of time."

"Did the woman die," says Sergeant Hall, and how in the hell did he get to New Orleans so fast."

"He is working with someone," says Lieutenant Towns. "And no, the woman did not die but she is severely traumatized."

Back in New Orleans the man called Marvin goes to Algiers and introduces himself as Michael Alexander and hangs out in the local nightspot called Algiers at night, a very lively place with dancing and pool tables and pretty locals drinking and partying the night away. Marvin, or Michael as he calls himself plays a game of pool with one of the locals and talks obnoxiously as he plays the game. A pretty white waitress takes the orders and Marvin orders a round for everyone. Marvin speaks very rudely to the waitress.

"Hurry the hell back with my order, he says, I don't like to be kept waiting. You white motherfuckers think y'all still in charge but y'all ain't runnin shit." The bar is mostly white but there are several nationalities in the bar and they are not comfortable with Marvin's conversation. Some of the men stare at Marvin as he continues to order food and drinks for everyone. Marvin misses a shot on the pool table and freaks out and slams the ball up against the wall and takes his pool stick and slams it on the table while pushing the rest of the balls in the pocket. The locals are upset with him and the owner of the club comes over to ask Marvin to pay his tab and leave.

"Sir I'm going to have to ask you to leave," says the owner with a bouncer, now get the fuck out of here."

"I've got to use the bathroom," says Marvin, then I'll pay and get out of here." Marvin heads to the bathroom in the crowded club and soon disappears in the crowd towards the restroom. The bouncer tries to locate Michael or Marvin but he is out of his view. Even in the crowd of people Marvin is bold as he grabs a woman near the bathroom and pulls her into the men's bathroom and into the stall with his hand wrapped around her mouth and tries to molest the woman in the crowded club. Marvin rips the woman's panties off while having a tight grip on her mouth as a few patrons near the bathroom run and grab the bouncer who rushes towards the bathroom to try and save the woman. Marvin continues to hold the woman with one hand while penetrating her at the same time. The bouncer bursts into the bathroom and heads towards the stall and Marvin releases the woman and opens the door forcefully slamming it against the head of the bouncer. At that point Marvin runs from the restroom and pulls a revolver from his waist and fires it right into the club.

9

People everyone start to scatter and in the commotion he flees the club hidden in the mass of humanity and runs away into the night. Masses of people are all over the streets not knowing where or who the gunman is and the wicked man jumps into an awaiting car and drives away. The members of the club reemerge to see what kind of damage has been caused and realize that the shot fired struck one of the employees and they call the paramedics along with the police. As the ambulance arrive they take the injured man to the hospital and speak to the owner and other members of the club.

"That was an angry man," says the owner, he is very, very dangerous. In the middle of a full club he drags a woman into the bathroom and damn near killed her and rapes her in the stall. He said his name was Michael Alexander, he looks polished on the outside but he has a demon inside of him".

The name Michael Alexander of course rings a bell because of what happened at the Hilton earlier and the New Orleans police realize they have a very dangerous predator in the city. The city is put on high alert and the FBI is alerted and DNA is taken from the bathroom along with fingerprints.

Back in Los Angeles Michael finally wakes up the next morning to the news that he is wanted for another serious crime in New Orleans and just in to the news room Michael Alexander is also wanted for a sexual assault and shooting in Algiers which is a suburb of New Orleans. Michael watches as many people attending the club that night describe the suspect and the fear they experienced at the sound of gunfire. As

Michael watches the television the other people in the home come into the room and watch with him as his name is being dragged through the mud.

"I will never be able to live this shit down ,says Michael, even if I clear my name it will never really be clear. Someone is trying to destroy me and they are doing a very good job."

"What's the connection with New Orleans," says officer Andrews, it seems like they've posted up there for now."

"Well we're going to find out," says Correta. "Everyone get your stuff together we are going to New Orleans. I told my pilot to prepare the plane because we're off as soon as everybody gets packed or whatever they need to do. I've hired a private detective and he will meet us in New Orleans and I've got my guard going with us so we will be protected until we get to the bottom of this."

"Am I going too?" asks Donald. "You know I can be a personal bodyguard for Cheryl. Any man would like to guard that body."

"You never give up do you, asks Cheryl, if I gave you a chance you couldn't handle it."

"Enough small talk," says Correta. "Let's get cracking and get out of here." Back at SOPD Sergeant Hall and Lieutenant Towns look at the news reports from New Orleans and realize that the investigation is getting much more complex.

"This fool going off the deep end," says Sergeant Hall, he's all the way in New Orleans killing and raping people. Everybody's looking for him and yet he keeps getting away.

I need Michael Alexander with me on my hide and go seek team." As Sergeant Hall and Lieutenant Towns talk Captain Joseph Hardy comes into the room.

"The mayor is really on my back about this Michael Alexander situation," says Captain Hardy, anything you can tell me about New Orleans."

"No sir," says Sergeant Hall, no more than what we see on the news."

"Well we don't want to be shut out of this," says Captain Hardy, a lot of his crimes are in our jurisdiction and I want his perverted ass. Hall, you and Towns head to New Orleans immediately. I've talked to people up there are they're willing to accept any help they can get. Fly out of here tonight, your itinerary and living arrangements are set. Don't come back here without Alexander." With that the Captain leaves the room and Hall and Towns make arrangements to leave the city. To make things more difficult is that the next day is July 4 and the New Orleans festival will be going on in and potentially 1 million new people will be in town.

So Coretta James heads to her Limo along with Michael and Cheryl and Donald and Officer Andrews. Coretta has several members of her security team along with her recently acquired bodyguard as they make their way to her private airfield to board her private jet and they head to New Orleans. On the other side of town Sergeant Hall and Lieutenant Towns head towards LAX for the 4 and ½ hour flight to New Orleans.

Back in New Orleans a man and a woman have a conversation in the French Quarter.

"Marvin, why are you taking all these unnecessary risks?" asks the woman. "That shit you did in Algiers last night was over the top."

"That's the best rush I had in a long time," says Marvin, besides they think my brother did it, and you shut the fuck up anyway and let me run the show. You just continue being my Coretta James, okay Doris. We get any calls today, anybody wants to spend some time with Michael Alexander."

"Nobody's going to call here now," says Doris, the whole nation is scared of the escort business."

"Yes, thanks to Michael Alexander," says Marvin, make some calls and see if you can set me up a date."

"Marvin," says Doris, we need to lay low and let it blow over a little bit until they arrest your brother again." Marvin grabs Doris around her mouth in a very tight grip and squeezes tight. Doris tries to break his grip but cannot move.

"You just do what the fuck I tell you to do," says Marvin, staring her in the face and finally releasing his grip, when I finish with my brother he is going to feel everything I felt and more. Now take off your clothes and after I finish with you, get on the phone and be Coretta." Marvin laughs loudly and Doris screams as he snatches her hair and gives her rough sex and she moans in pain and endures his normal humiliating words as he degrades her.

CHAPTER 38

NEW ORLEANS BOUND

That afternoon Coretta's jet arrives at an airfield on the outskirts of New Orleans and Coretta and her entourage jump into three awaiting cars and head towards Canal street in the heart of New Orleans. Coretta has rented adjoining cottages on Canal right from the French Quarter under an assumed name and the convoy heads in that direction. Soon afterwards Lieutenant Towns and Sergeant Hall arrive at Louis Armstrong International Airport in New Orleans and after going to the baggage claim they pick up their rented car and head towards Canal street and the Hilton hotel to stay in the same Hotel where Tina Miller was assaulted. The three groups of people, Michael and Coretta, Marvin and Doris and Sergeant Hall and Lieutenant Towns are all staying within a mile of each other and they all embrace for the upcoming events.

Back in Coretta's entourage Michael and Donald are admiring the sights of the New Orleans festival as they ride to their rented homes.

"Shit," says Donald, I haven't seen this kind of talent in a long time. Black women are the finest women in the world by far. Everywhere you look you see a 10 or a 12, do they have this shit every year."

"Yea man," says Michael. "I came one time in college, the parties up here are unreal. Right now in the middle of the day you can go into any bar down here and party your ass off."

"Yea Michael," says Cheryl. "Sheila and I came once in college, we left you and Ken behind. We had the time of our lives."

"You brought my wife up here without me knowing?" asks Michael. "Did she enjoy herself?"

"She wasn't your wife yet," says Cheryl. "And yes she let her hair down a little bit. But all she talked about the whole weekend was you."

"Yea so you say," says Michael. "You can tell me the real."

The streets are packed and the group finally maneuvers its way through the crowd onto the adjoining streets to the rented houses. Michael, Coretta, Officer Andrews, Donald and Cheryl take the first house and Coretta's security team take the second home and set up house. Michael looks at the concert lineup in the first house and can't believe the talent.

"Janet Jackson, Eve and look Erykah Badu," says Michael. "I would to Badu Erykah Badu, that woman is so fine to me."

"I don't think you can handle that Michael," says Correta. "She turns a lot of brothers out. She has them losing their mind."

"I want to be turned out," says Michael. "But you know, that's what good about the festival, you don't need to go to the concerts. There are so many stars walking up and down the streets that you don't even think about a concert. The best party I went to in my life was at 12 noon in a bar on Canal during the festival, this shit is unreal."

As Michael and crew talk about the New Orleans festival Sergeant Hall and Lieutenant Towns have checked into their rooms and are greeted by members of the NOPD and they check out the room where Tina Miller was assaulted and then they view the tapes of what they believe is Michael Alexander fleeing the scene of the crime.

"It's amazing he could not only escape from jail but also make his way to New Orleans and commit this assault," says Sergeant Hall, I've never seen anything like it." As they look at the tape Lieutenant Towns makes an observation.

"That's definitely him, she says , do you have any idea where he may be hiding."

"With the events going on in the city," says a Detective from New Orleans, he could be hiding anywhere, maybe in plain sight. I'm sure he thought about the events in the city before he came up here. It's kind of the perfect storm for a criminal but he will make a mistake, the man is the boldest criminal I've ever seen."

"We're going to walk the streets," says Sergeant Hall, I guarantee you he is going to be right in the middle of the action." Sergeant Hall and Lieutenant Towns leave the Hotel and just walk the streets in the midst of the Festival party and hope they run into Michael Alexander.

Back at Marvin and Doris's hideaway Marvin is just finishing up his brutal sexcapade with Doris and decides to just walk the streets and Doris reminds Marvin of his plight.

"Marvin don't forget to take your phone ,says a submissive Doris, if anything comes up I will call you, and make sure you keep your eyes open because everybody is looking for you."

"I know what I'm doing Doris, yells Marvin, you get set me up a client, you know how much the women love me."

"Yea I know," whispers Doris," they can't wait to see you." Marvin boldly walks out of the residence and heads towards the French Quarter towards the bar area.

Sergeant Hall and Lieutenant Towns walk up and down the bar area showing pictures of Michael Alexander to the people on the streets and they post up in various areas of the scene and look at all the people walking by and they see several men that resemble Michael only for it to be a false alarm.

"If I wasn't up here on duty," says Sergeant Hall, I would really enjoy this, this is my kind of crowd."

"Yea if you are into this kind of superficial stuff," says Lieutenant Towns. "Never thought of you as being such a shallow person."

"It's not shallow Lieutenant, he says , I just like to see beautiful people having a good time."

Right up the block from the Detectives, Marvin Williams walks around grabbing on the women and throwing caution to the wind. Marvin grabs a woman right in front of her man and the man confronts Marvin.

"Motherfucker did you just grab my woman, asks the man I'll fuck you up." Marvin just looks at the man and tries to walk off. The man pushes Marvin and tells him he is about to get his ass whipped. Marvin pulls out his .38 revolver and puts it in the man's face right in front of a crowd of people and grabs the man by his hair.

"You don't know who you're fucking with," says Marvin sticking the gun to the man's nose, I'll blow your motherfucking face off right in front of your girl. Get on your knees bitch." As Marvin holds the gun to the man's face another man runs to Sergeant Hall and yells to him.

"The man you're looking for is right over there," says the man pointing to Marvin, he's about to shoot to shoot that man in front of his girl." The two Detectives look up and see the man on his knees with a gun to his face and they immediately draw their weapons. Marvin looks up and sees the two Detectives coming towards him and runs full speed through the crowd.

"Police, yells Sergeant Hall, drop your weapon.

"Police," says Lieutenant Towns. "Stop." Marvin runs through the crowd knocking people over trying to run away from the officers. The crowd of people in the streets start to scream as Marvin runs with his gun exposed chased by the two officers.

"Get down, yells Sergeant Hall as he tries to get a shot at Marvin, get down." Marvin bobs and weaves through the crowd of people and runs into the Hilton Hotel, the same

Hotel that he attacked Tina Miller in chased by the two Detectives. The Detectives yell at the people in the Hotel.

"Stop that man, yell the detectives, get down everybody." A man moves toward Marvin and he shoots the man point blank and heads for the side exit running full speed. Lieutenant Towns stops to assist the injured man as Sergeant Hall continues to chase Marvin out the exit and as he reaches the street he no longer sees Marvin running. The Sergeant slowly walks around the corridor of the building and doesn't see Marvin but he continues to look for him. Sergeant Hall looks in the building next door and cannot find Marvin, whom he believes is Michael. The people in the building are alarmed to see the detective with his gun drawn. On the other side of the building Marvin looks to see the detective has gone the other direction and heads back towards his hideaway that he shares with Doris and he reaches the apartment in a panic but felling exhilarated. Marvin opens the door sweating profusely and in a panic.

"What happened," says Doris, why are you sweating like that?"

"I just got chased by two punk ass cops, he says, I thought they were gonna catch me." Marvin sits down on the sofa and starts laughing and his demeanor suddenly changes.

"What a rush," says Marvin, that was fun." Doris looks at Marvin and realizes again what an idiot he is.

"Those fools almost caught me, yells Marvin, my heart is beating like a racehorse." He sits down and tries to relax.

"Bring me a drink, yells Marvin, I need to calm down."

CHAPTER 39

A BOLD KILLER

As Marvin sits down and revels in his perceived glory, Sergeant Hall returns to the Hilton and sees the crowd around the injured man. People try to revive the man who was shot point blank between the eyes and Lieutenant Towns stands up covered in blood and delivers the bad news.

"He's dead," she states, "he probably died instantly. Did you see where the suspect went?"

"No," says Sergeant Hall, that fool got away, I have no idea which way he ran." An ambulance tries to come between the large crowd of onlookers and New Orleans festival people and go into the Hotel to try to help the victim and then transport his body to the morgue. The detectives feel as though they have caused the innocent man's death and feel somber about the situation but they are more determined than ever to apprehend Michael Alexander.

At house number 1 with Coretta, Michael, Cheryl and Officer Andrews, Cheryl is trying to prepare dinner for everyone and she needs some olive oil and she sends Michael and Donald to a store that is right next door to their house along with one of Coretta's protection team. The store is directly across the street from the house so Michael feels somewhat safe although Coretta and Cheryl advise him against going and Officer Andrews also decides to tag along. Although there is a buzz on Canal street from the excitement involving Marvin, they are oblivious to the commotion. They enter the store looking for olive oil only. Coretta's security person receives a call from her telling him that she has news for Michael and they grab the olive oil and head for the counter. Beautiful women are all over the place and Michael and Donald are looking left and right. Donald gets to the register to pay for the olive oil and the clerk says the olive oil is $10 and Donald freaks.

"Ten Dollars for Olive oil," says Donald, when did olive oil get so expensive."

"It's not expensive," says the clerk, it's that extra virgin olive oil, it costs more."

"Virgin olive oil," says Donald, you got any of that hoeish, extra freaky olive oil, you know the kind that hangs out at night."

"Hoeish olive oil," says the clerk, your ass just cheap."

"I'm not too cheap to put my foot in your ass," says Donald, don't let the smooth taste fool you." Michael grabs Donald and takes the olive oil and heads back to the house as Coretta greets them coming in the door.

"Michael," says Correta. "The private detective that I hired says there's a man in the ninth ward that says he recognizes the man committing the crimes and he says it's not you, at least the name doesn't match, he said he is willing to meet with us. I think you should go so that he can see you and be able to testify for us in court. Take one of my guards with you and Officer Andrews, my security person has the address and he is ready whenever you are."

"Can I go too?" asks Donald. "I can make him give us all the info."

"No," says Cheryl. "You just stay with me and help me make this stir fry. They see you and they won't think we are serious, besides you can help me cook." Donald loves the idea of hanging out with Cheryl while Michael, Officer Andrews and Coretta's guard head towards the Ninth Ward to speak to the man.

Back in the house holding Marvin and Doris, Marvin is feeling antsy and wants to calm down.

"Doris," says Marvin, roll me up a blunt and lace it with some coke. How much money we got left from that million I got when I smoked that stupid ass Limo driver, that fool thought he was on easy street. Now his dumb ass laying on a cold hard slab." Doris rolls a blunt and grabs her pipe for herself and while Marvin smokes his blunt she indulges in her crack pipe. Doris was a very beautiful statuesque sister but after years of dealing with Marvin and doing drugs the woman looks frail and tired and no matter what abuse Marvin puts her through she remains loyal to him. After smoking his blunt laced with cocaine Marvin wants to get back out on the streets he barely escaped a few moments ago. Doris gets a high from her crack pipe and after smoking it she wants more and she looks on the floor and sees something white and she thinks it is crack and she picks it up.

" That's lint," says Marvin, you got it bad."

Doris tries to convince Marvin of the detriment of going back to the French Quarter and Canal street.

"I'm going back out to the French Quarter to see some sights and have a few drinks with my peers," says Marvin."

"Marvin it's not worth the risk," says Doris, let's just sit here and get fucked up, we still have plenty of cash left and we can just chill."

"You mind your own damn business," says Marvin, they can't catch me and even if they do I'm invincible. Besides you can't even tell the difference between lint and crack. I'm like the gang brothers, I don't die I just multiply." Marvin is as high as a kite and steps out of his place boldly and walks back down to the French Quarter as if it is a stroll in the park. Doris grabs her 9 millimeter revolver and walks out of the house behind him and tries to keep up. The inebriated Marvin walks out of the house and heads directly to a bar on the south corner of Canal street and goes into the bar and orders a drink in the midst of the crowd. He stumbles his way through the crowd pulling on women and he orders a Long Island Ice Tea and stands boldly as if the women are checking him out. His eyes are red as fire and the pressures of his life are written all over his face. As the waitress brings back his drink Marvin spills his drink on a man who takes a look at his face and remembers his face from TV and also remembers him from earlier with the two detectives and the man whispers to his friend.

"That looks like that rapist from TV," says the man, I remember him from earlier when that man got shot in the Hilton." The word goes around the bar about who Marvin potentially is and several men decide to try and grab him and hold him for the police. The men in the bar start to stare at Marvin and he can feel the tension and he starts to go into his pants and grab his gun when two black men grab him from behind and several other men attack him from the front and side. They drag Marvin from the club believing him to be Michael Alexander. "Its that rapist motherfucker Michael Alexander, yells one of the men, drag his ass out into the streets. Somebody go call the police. "As a few men run and seek out the police several men kick Marvin and taunt him and also punch him. The crowd starts to turn into a small mob when a light but definitive voice pierces the crowd.

"Get the fuck off him," says Doris pointing her .9 millimeter gun right at the hostile crowd, I said get the fuck off him," she yells. The men quickly back away and Marvin pulls his gun but Doris dissuades him from pulling the trigger.

"Come on Marvin we got to get out of here, she says, come on let's go." Doris and Marvin rush up the street and a few moments later several men come back with the New Orleans police officers. Lieutenant Towns and Sergeant Hall

are walking around The French Quarter and run towards the
sound of hysteria.

" What happened, asks Sergeant Hall to a man standing
by, what's all the commotion."

"They had that rapist Michael Alexander caught and they
were stomping his ass on the ground," says the man, when
some woman comes up and pulls a gun on the crowd and she
saved his ass."

"Could be that Attorney," says Sergeant Hall, or that
Madam Coretta James. Her name has been linked with him
in the last couple of days."

"This woman looked bad," says the man, she looked like
she was high on some shit."

"Which way did they run?" asks Sergeant Hall, point me
the right way." The man points in the direction Marvin and
Doris ran towards and the two detectives head that direction.
As the police search Marvin and Doris are able to weave
their way through the Festival crowd and they need a plan. A
delivery van pulls up in front of the building where the two
of them are standing and Marvin quickly pounces pulling
his gun from his pocket and sticking it directly in the young
drivers face, a white male in his mid twenties.

"Give me that van white boy," says Marvin as he pistol
whips the young man, get the fuck out of here." Marvin jumps
in the van and Doris gets in the passenger seat and the two
of them take off.

"We need to find some where to lay low," says Marvin, it's
too much heat down here."

"I told you not to take your ass back in those streets," says Doris, why you gotta always test the boundaries?"

"Shut the hell up," says Marvin, I do what the fuck I want to do. Shit let's head to the old neighborhood, the ninth ward. We can stash this van and get the hell out of the city."

CHAPTER 40

SECRETS REVEALED

As Marvin and Doris make their way to the ninth ward Coretta gets a visit from her private detective who has some startling news for her.

"Ms. James I did some digging and look what I came up with," says the Private Detective, this is the original birth certificate for Michael Alexander." Coretta takes a look at the birth certificate and her mouth flies open.

"This is unbelievable," says Correta. "Two of them. Michael said he didn't have a brother."

"Maybe he doesn't know ,says the private detective, I'm sure he doesn't have this copy of his birth certificate and maybe he is just as much in the dark as we are." Across the way Cheryl eves drops on the conversation and puts her hand over her mouth.

"This explains a lot of things," says Correta. "What about the mother."

"I talked to her and told her what I found," says the Private Detective, she's on a plane now headed for New Orleans. I think she has some explaining to do to her son. We need to pick her up within the hour."

"Okay get my security team," says Correta. "We need to take off ASAP."

"I'm coming too," says Cheryl. "I want to be there for Michael."

"No," says Correta. "Stay here with Donald and we'll be back."

"I'm going whether you like it or not," says Cheryl. "Try and stop me from getting in the car." Coretta approaches Cheryl.

"I've had about enough of your mouth," says Correta. "It's time I put you in your place." Coretta draws back and slaps Cheryl in the face and knocks her back as Donald looks on from across the way. Cheryl doesn't hesitate to regroup and slaps Coretta back as her security team enters the room.

"Damn, this kind of shit don't even happen in the movies," says Donald watching intently. The team looks at Coretta and waits for her command and she does nothing. Coretta has never had anyone to stand up to her like that and actually respects Cheryl.

"Ok," says Coretta to Cheryl softly while rubbing her face, I guess you can go." The group gets into Coretta's rented black Suburban and heads towards Louis Armstrong Airport.

While that was going on Michael and Officer Andrews along with a member of Coretta's security team arrive at the address in the Ninth Ward near the infamous St. Claude and Florida street. An older somewhat run down house on the corner is where the address leads them. Sitting in front of the house is an old man named Terry McCall and he jumps up when he sees Michael.

"Marvin," says the man, you're sure looking good these days." Michael looks back at the man.

"That's the second time somebody has called me Marvin," says Michael. "Who the hell is Marvin and why do people keep calling me that."

"You know they say everybody has a twin," says Terry McCall, well Marvin is your twin and the two of you look just alike. But now that I look at you I can see the difference, Marvin never dresses that well, not unless he is trying to con somebody." "Are you the man that reported that he knew the rapist, asks Officer Andrews, you think he is this Marvin Williams."

"I'm sure of it," says the man, his daddy big Marv was my best friend back in the day. Get me a bottle of Scotch and I'll tell you the whole story."

"Scotch," says Officer Andrews, Scotch." Michael waves at Officer Andrews.

"Where the liquor store old man?" asks Michael. "What kind of Scotch you drink?"

"My name is Terry not old man," says Terry, and this is the hood, there's a liquor store on every corner." Sure enough Michael looks directly across and a liquor store is right there on the corner.

"Alright I'll be right back," says Michael, Michael goes to the liquor and buys a bottle of McCallum 21 and brings it back.

"You bought some good shit," says Terry pulling out two glasses, I never drink by myself." The man pours Michael a drink and starts to talk.

"Big Marv raised that boy Marvin by himself," says Terry, I never knew who his mother was. They were doing good here until Katrina, that shit tore up this whole neighborhood. I saw a woman trapped on her house and before someone could reach her she drowned right here on the streets. Big Marv and his son lived right over there next door to me and they would always come over and hang out with me, we were all close. Marvin Jr. was a smart boy, good athlete, good looking young man. And then when the hurricane hit they lost everything, they had to move to Houston and he eventually ended going to jail, Big Marv would call me and tell me that boy had changed, something was wrong with him."

"Why did he go to jail, asked Michael, what did he do."

"He robbed a liquor store in Houston," says Terry, he did ten years and that's hard time. But something happened to him before he went to jail. Big Marv would call me and tell me that one day the boy just changed. He became withdrawn, was rude to everybody, even him. He said the boy started killing and torturing animals, any animals, dogs, cats, squirrels, anything. He would mutilate the animals and hang them in a shed Marv had built out in the back of their house."

As the man talks Marvin and Doris pull up right across from them and see the men talking and recognizes the old man and his brother Michael. Marvin comes close to try and hear the conversation in his old stomping grounds.

"Big Marv tried everything to save that boy," says Terry while sipping on a scotch, he spent thousands of dollars on psychiatrists and all kinds of professionals but the boy never revealed what happened to him. And then one day I lost communication with Big Marv, it was like he vanished off the face of the earth."

"What about his son," says Officer Andrews, you ever see him again."

"From time to time," says Terry, he would come through the old neighborhood sometimes. That boy is sick, when I would see him coming I would step to the side, he argued and fought with everybody and the only person that could deal with him was Doris Washington, she crushed on him when he was young and remained in contact with him all the way. I bet she's still with him now even though he beats the hell out of her. She's from the Ninth Ward too."

"You got any idea where they would be," says Officer Andrews, we need to find them."

"They could be anywhere in New Orleans," says Terry, Doris is a junkie and Marvin probably is too, they could be anywhere." As they talk Marvin stands not far away out of sight listening to the conversation. Terry takes another hard look at Michael.

"Come to think of it, says Terry, that's got to be your real brother because you look exactly like Marvin, same hair, same nose, same mouth. Somebody, somewhere is withholding some information from you."

"Mr. McCall," says Michael. "If I had a twin brother I would know it. Why would my parents keep that from me?"

Terry starts to speak French to Michael.

"Je Suis désolé mon ami mais tu as un frère jumeau," says Terry.

"What does that mean good brother?" asks Michael.

"It means I'm sorry my friend but you have a twin brother, "says Terry. Michael and Officer Andrews just look at each other and Coretta's security continues to survey the area as Marvin and Doris listen in but try to dodge the alert guard.

"Let's go Michael," says Officer Andrews, that's a lot of hearsay and we need more."

"Spend something with me," says Terry, I need to pay the taxes on my house." Michael hands the man $500 dollars which is all he has and wishes him goodbye and the three of them start to leave.

"I'll call you when this is over and do more for you sir," says Michael. "It's been a pleasure." Michael and his comrades leave and Marvin comes from his hiding place and walks up behind Terry with his gun drawn.

"You talk too much old man," says Marvin. Marvin surprisingly does not shoot Terry.

"Come on Doris," says Marvin, let's follow them and see where they lead us. I've played games long enough with my brother, it's time for me to get out of New Orleans and I need to put my brother out of his misery."

CHAPTER 41

MICHAEL MEETS MARVIN

Coretta and her entourage arrive at Louis Armstrong airport and they pick up Michael's mother at the front of the terminal and after putting her bag in the truck they take off. "Hello Mrs. Alexander," says Correta. "My name is Coretta James and these are members of my security team and I think you have already spoken to my Private Detective over the phone.

"Hi Mrs. Alexander," says Cheryl. "It's good to see you again."

"Hello, Cheryl," says Michael's mom, it's good to see you again."

"Mrs Alexander," says Correta. "I'm sure my Detective already informed you that we found a copy of Michael's original birth certificate and we noticed something very interesting, Michael has a twin brother named Marvin." Mrs. Alexander just listens but doesn't speak.

"And I am also sure that you are aware that your son Michael has been accused of some hideous things," says Coretta speaking like an Attorney, things that none of us believe he is capable."

"No," says Mrs. Alexander, Michael would never even think about doing such things."

"What about Marvin, asks Cheryl cutting in, is Marvin capable of such things." Mrs. Alexander doesn't speak.

"You see my Detective spoke with several medical officials," says Correta. "And the only two people that share DNA are identical twins. So either Michael or Marvin committed these crimes. So who do you think did it Mrs. Alexander."

Michael's mother gives Coretta an evil look.

"How is it that your son's don't know about each other, asks Cheryl, how is that possible."

Mrs Alexander hesitates and looks down.

"Marvin knows about Michael," says Mrs. Alexander, Michael just doesn't know about Marvin."

"Why?" asks Cheryl tag teaming with Coretta.

"I need to speak to Michael before I say anymore," says Mrs. Alexander.

As Coretta and Cheryl question Michael's mother officer Andrews and Michael talk in the car.

"Well Michael," says Officer Andrews, I just googled my phone and it said something very interesting. There is only one possible scenario where people share DNA and that is identical twins, not fraternal twins, not brothers and sisters, identical twins and identical twins only. The only thing they don't share are their fingerprints."

"Man my mother has never lied to me in my life," says Michael. "I always wished for a brother, do you think she would keep that from me?"

"Maybe she didn't know," says Officer Andrews," many children are taken at birth. You need to get on the horn and talk to your mother." As Michael and Officer Andrews talk Coretta's security man in the car gets a phone call. He answers the phone then hands it directly to Michael.

"Hello Michael," says the voice on the phone, how are you son."

"Mom," says Michael. "Where are you, is something wrong with Brittany."

"No," says Michael's mom, she is with my sister. I'm in New Orleans with Coretta James and your friend Cheryl, we need to talk son."

"Mom," says Michael. "Put Coretta on the phone." Michael's mom hands Coretta the phone.

"Why do you have my mom?" asks Michael. "Why do you have my mom?"

"She just flew in," says Correta. "She needs to talk to you and it needs to be now. Ask my security where you are now." Michael asks the security who says they are near a high rise called Place St. Charles.

"Good," says Correta. "Go there and with all the events going on in the city take the elevator all the way to the top and go to the roof, were on our way." Coretta hangs up the phone and Michael and crew head towards Place St. Charles.

"My mother is in town and she says she needs to speak to me immediately," says Michael. "What's up with that."

"Maybe your mama got a secret to tell you," says Coretta security, sound like mama been burning the midnight cable."

219

Michael is shocked by the security officer who has been professional up to that point.

"Watch your fucking mouth bitch," says Michael as he slaps Coretta's security hard on the arm. "Don't make me pull this car over," says Security, don't let your mouth write a check your ass can't cash"

"You say something else about my mother and we're gonna find out," says Michael. "You better drive this car like a good little hired hand."

"I ain't Coretta, she's sprung on you, boy," says Security, you don't have me on a string, I'll whup your fucking ass. I don't like your punk ass anyway. I didn't like you 5 years ago, I was in the cut when all that stuff was going on, you just didn't know it."

"Come on brothers," says Officer Andrews, we got other fish to fry."

"That's cool," says Security, but after this I'm gonna fry his ass."

"Fuck you and the horse you rode in on," says Michael. "I'm easy to find."

As the men argue in the car Marvin and Doris follow closely behind in their car because Marvin is not planning on leaving town without his brother's scalp. Michael, Officer Andrews and Coretta's security guard pull up in front of the Place St. Charles and Michael and the security exit and head towards each other. Officer Andrews steps in between the two men and tries to keep the peace. Coretta's security man is 6ft 4in tall and 215lbs and a black belt but Michael doesn't care.

"We'll finish this," says security, be careful what you ask for."

Parked across the way is Marvin Williams and his puppet Doris and Michael and Officer Andrews and Coretta's security ride up to the 53rd floor and exit and walk the stairway to the roof and wait for the others to come. Outside Marvin and Doris exit the car and a police officer recognizes Marvin and calls in backup as Marvin and Doris take the elevator to the top. A few moments later Coretta arrives with Michael's mother, Cheryl and the rest of Coretta's security team. There are revelations that need to come out and the repercussions will be explosive. The entourage with Coretta take the elevator to the 53rd floor and then they walk up to the top floor where Michael, Officer Andrews and Coretta's headstrong security person are up top waiting. Hiding in the hall of the 53rd floor is Marvin and Doris waiting to see what is going on with the group. As Coretta's crew reaches the top the hot summer air blows and the height of the building brings fear to those who are afraid of heights. Michael sees his mother and immediately goes to embrace her as everyone watches.

"Mom," says Michael. "What's going on, why are you here."

"I have to tell you something Michael," says Mrs. Alexander." As the woman starts to speak Marvin and Doris make their way to the top unbeknownst to the others.

Mama," says Marvin too himself.

"Michael," says his mother, I should have told you this a long time ago. Your father and I were having major problems, he was a good man but he was always gone. He was always being sent to one war after another and he would be gone for months if not years at a time and I was lonely and sometimes vulnerable. You know he was a Marine and he was so serious about his work, so I tried to stay strong. I was always close to his family and his first cousin Marvin would always come over and help, he would take me where I needed to go and he would do all the work around the house, cut the grass and fix things when I needed them and we became very close."

As Michael's mother talks all eyes are fixated on her including Marvin who remains out of sight. Michael looks on in amazement. Mrs. Alexander pauses as she continues to tell the story.

"I only wanted to go out sometimes," says Michael mother Mrs. Alexander, and Marvin would sometimes take me to the local watering holes and I would have a good time, it was totally innocent at first. But then my birthday came and your father didn't even call and I was hurt and vulnerable and then Marvin called and said he would take me out for my birthday and I had fun, and for a time I forgot about your father and when we got home it just happened, before I knew it, it just happened."

"What just happened Mom?" asks Michael. "You slept with your husband's first cousin?"

"Yes," says Mrs. Alexander, I slept with his cousin and I became pregnant. I didn't know what to do and I was confused. Marvin asked me to leave your father and be with him but he knew I wasn't in love with him, I was still in love with your father. When I told your father I was pregnant he was so excited and he didn't even consider that the timing was not right for him to be the father, he was on top of the world. He came back home but then he had to go to Japan and I found out I was having twins. All the time while this was going on Marvin kept pressuring me to tell your father that the babies were his, he said he would tell your father himself." While Michael's mother is speaking the New Orleans Police have surrounded the high rise and Sergeant Hall and Lieutenant Towns have also found their way to the site and have exited their cars and are trying to find out where Michael is in the building.

"Mom," says Michael. "What did you do?"

"I made a deal with Marvin," says Michael's mom, he agreed not to tell your father if I allowed him to raise one of the children, whichever child was born first he would take and I would keep the other. Your brother Marvin was born first and I allowed him to raise Marvin and I kept you. Your father was still overseas during the birth and of course he never knew of the arrangement, I ended up with you purely by chance and I made him promise that he would never tell your father. I didn't want to give away my child but I had no choice."

"Mom," says Michael. "You should have told dad, he would have been hurt of course but he deserved to know."

"I couldn't do that Michael," says Mrs. Alexander, your father would have never forgiven me, the last thing you could tell a man is that his children aren't really his and that your children are really your first cousins, he would have probably killed me and his cousin, so I kept my mouth shut."

"So did you ever talk to Marvin?" asks Michael. "Did you ever interact with your son?"

"No Michael," says his mother, Big Marvin would call me periodically and let me know how the boy was doing but I never talked to him, I just saw pictures." As Michael and his mother interact Marvin listens and gets more upset. At the bottom of the high rise several people report seeing people going up the elevator to the top floor and the police head towards that direction.

"So mom," says Michael. "I have a twin brother and daddy died never knowing that I wasn't really his son and that you really had twins. Mom how could you do that to dad, to me, to Marvin."

"I had no choice Michael, once I made the decision I couldn't turn back. Can't you see it was too late."

"It's never too late mom," says Michael. "Now look what's happened, people are chasing me all over the country for crimes I did not commit and worse than that it looks like my brother that I never knew is trying to put his crimes on me, you could have stopped this mom."

At that moment, as if coming out nowhere, Marvin walks out onto the roof and everyone looks in amazement, especially Michael who sees the twin he just recently heard of, in the flesh, it is like looking in a mirror. Cheryl's mouth is open and even the steel of Coretta is broken as she gawks at Marvin.

"Hello mother," says Marvin very rudely, glad to finally make your acquaintance." Marvin walks up to his brother Michael and just stares at him and Michael stares back.

"So how does it feel Michael to know that you have a brother?" says Marvin, kind of blows your mind doesn't it." Michael is at a loss for words and is still in amazement.

"Unlike Mama, my daddy told me a lot about you Michael," says Marvin, the years you played basketball, your style, the way he looked at your pictures and spoke about your accomplishments, he worshiped the ground you walked on, even though he never actually met you. He didn't look at me the same way and I was right there with him, I was a nerd, I never had a mother or a brother to turn to and daddy wasn't always there. He would be gone for days and leave me with friends and even strangers. But guess what happened Michael, he left me one time with a friend of his, a man I called Uncle Bob. Uncle Bob always bought me gifts and made me feel special and cooked for me, but guess what, Uncle Bob had a secret, he liked little boys. And guess what happened Michael, one day over to Uncle Bob's, when I was 11 years old, Uncle Bob raped me, do you hear that Michael, he fucked me in the ass. So while you were off playing basketball overseas I was losing my mind and I wondered how my twin brother didn't feel my pain, how he didn't know I existed."

"I'm sorry Marvin," says Michael. "I don't know what to say, I wish I would have known."

"You should have known," says Marvin, and then when I started getting in trouble daddy was about to come find you. I guess he wanted to replace his fucked up son with his golden child son. And I couldn't let that happen Michael so I made daddy permanently disappear, I did you a favor Michael. After that I just wanted you to suffer, the same way I suffered, because twins are supposed to bear each others burdens. And then I discovered DNA, identical twins have the same DNA, did you know that Michael, well, anyway, I just used your lifestyle against you. Oh, I'm sorry, excuse my rudeness, this is Donna, this is my Coretta James."

"She don't look nothing like me," says Correta. "Girl go get your weave fixed or something." Coretta's security team is ready to strike at the drop of a hat and are on high alert. Marvin has his gun sticking out of his pants in plain sight to all but has not yet made a threatening move. Doris just stands and watches Marvin and Michael and although the brothers are identical looking their differences are obvious.

CHAPTER 42

TIME TO PAY THE PIPER

At that moment the New Orleans police reach the roof with guns drawn followed by Lieutenant Towns and Sergeant Hall with guns drawn and Marvin pulls his gun and Coretta's men also pull their weapons and Michael is weaponless in the middle standing near his heartbroken mother. Sergeant Hall and Lieutenant Towns can't believe what they see, two Michaels.

"That explains the fingerprints," says Lieutenant Towns. "This can't be real."

"Fingerprints, what fingerprints," says Sergeant Hall, I thought the fingerprints came back as Mr. Alexanders." Sergeant Hall stares at Lieutenant Towns.

"Who else knows about this? asks Sergeant Hall. "And why did you keep it from me?"

"The DA knows," says Lieutenant Towns. "We agreed that the fingerprints didn't matter as long as the DNA matched."

"What," says Sergeant Hall, the fingerprints always matter." Michael overhears the conversation and can't believe his ears.

"You dirty bitch," says Michael. "You mean you knew the fingerprints didn't match mines and you didn't acknowledge it. That's against the law isn't it."

"It don't matter anyway," says Lieutenant Towns. " You did it. I should kill your ass." Sergeant Hall removes the gun from Lieutenant Towns and removes her from the situation.

"Now will someone tell me what's going on here," says Sergeant Hall, am I seeing double."

"Sergeant Hall," says Michael. "Meet my brother Marvin, my identical twin brother."

"Identical twin," says Sergeant Hall, where he come from."

"I don't know," says Michael. "I just met him for the first time today."

"I'm sorry Mama," says Marvin, but I have to do this.? Marvin pulls the gun from his pocket and is about to shoot his mother but Michael steps in the way.

"No, yells Michael, don't kill my mother." The police and security officers have their guns aimed at Marvin.

"Drop that shit or you a dead motherfucker, yells Sergeant Hall, now." Marvin just stands still and can't believe his eyes.

"You would die for her after what she did to us," says Marvin to Michael, she fucked up our lives."

"I'm sorry what happened to you," says Michael. "I really am, but the things you're doing now is because you choose to do them, and you're setting me up for the fall. What did you want, for me to get raped in jail because you were molested."

"Exactly," says Marvin, twins are supposed to share everything. I wanted you to share the pain I felt because that's what we are supposed to do, brothers share." Marvin has a serious but crazy stare on his face as he speaks and the police look with guns drawn and Donna standing back waiting in fear.

"I'm sorry my brother," says Michael. "But that's one thing I don't want to share with you or anybody else. I'm truly sorry about what happened to you, I know you lost a lot but as long as you're alive you have a chance."

"I have no chance," says Marvin, look at all these guns on me." Marvin lifts his gun up and puts it to his own head and walks through the crowd towards the edge of the building and steps up on the edge of the high rise.

"You don't have to do this, says Sergeant Hall, come down brother we can work this."

"Marvin please come down," says Mrs. Alexander, we can work this out together."

"Please Marvin," says Doris, please." Michael walks towards him.

"Come on," says Michael. "It's not too late for us to be brothers."

"It's too late for that," says Marvin, "and just for the record I would never kill myself." Marvin pulls the gun down from his head and tries to aim it at Michael and shots go off from everywhere and Marvin yells and falls from the roof of the 53 story building. Michael, his mother and Karen all yell no at the same time as Marvin falls.

Michael's mother screams in pain and Karen pulls her gun and shoots herself and drops like a rock to the ground. Michael just holds his head down as his mother continues to scream and Cheryl grabs Michael tightly and tries to comfort him as he openly weeps and thinks about what could have been. Michael stands up and looks over the roof and tries to see his brother.

"I don't see him," says Michael. "But that is a long way down." Michael sees blood from the gunshots on the edge and the reality of the situation slaps him in the face. Michael is as sad as he has ever been in his life as his mother sobs uncontrollably and the police call for other units to go and retrieve Marvin's body. Sergeant Hall admonishes Lieutenant Towns and approaches Michael.

"I'm not going to arrest you because I don't believe you committed these crimes after what I have seen and heard today," says Sergeant Hall, but don't run anymore until we sort all of this stuff out. I apologize for Lieutenant Towns, she put her personal feelings before professionalism. You better take care of your mom." Michael goes over and tries to lift his mother off the floor but she crumbles to the ground as if she is lifeless. Coretta has her security assist and they eventually work their way away from the scene. As the entourage leaves the building they expect to see Marvin's mangled body on the sidewalk but thankfully for Michael and his mother the body is nowhere to be found.

CHAPTER 43

CORETTA'S SCHEME

Later that evening as the entourage heads back to Los Angeles on Coretta's jet, Michael sits alone on the plane when Coretta approaches him and tries to console him.

"I'm sorry Michael," says Correta. "I can't imagine what you are feeling right now."

"I really don't know how I feel," says Michael. "Finding out that I had a brother all these years and knowing that my mother kept it from me, it really hurts. And most of all, knowing my father died not knowing I wasn't really his son. But that was my dad, no matter what the DNA says."

"I agree Michael," says Correta. "The man took care of you all your life and he loved you unconditionally, that's your dad! And Michael you know I did everything that I could for you, I spent my money and gave it my all."

"Yes you did," says Michael, "and I can't thank you enough, and if there's anything I can ever do to repay you I will do it, no questions asked."

"Well Michael, I'm glad you feel that way," says Correta. "Because I need a favor."

"Uh-oh," says Michael. "Do I want to hear this? No more dancing in front of transvestites I hope!"

"No nothing like that," says Correta. "But I do need your masculine services. Ava Jones, a good friend and a very successful and very beautiful designer from Dallas is in town and she wants to meet you."

"What," says Michael. "Coretta after what I just went through, you expect me to spend time with one of your clients, come on. And besides, I don't do that anymore and I haven't done it for years." "You just said anything I need," says Correta. "I need this Michael. She is only in town for the night and as beautiful as she is she has a hard time meeting men."

"You mean tonight," says Michael. "I'm exhausted." "Just give her an hour Michael," says Correta. "She is staying downtown in a suite near the Staple Center and if you give her an hour that will be all she needs."

"One hour?," says Michael.

"One," says Correta. "She just needs to be held." "What about mom," says Michael. "She needs me now."

"Cheryl and I can take care of your mom until you get back," says Correta. "I will have a separate driver there to take you to her suite and bring you home, it will be painless." Michael reluctantly agrees as Cheryl looks on from a distance, suspicious of Coretta but not being able to hear their conversation. Coretta leaves Michael and goes into the cabin of the plane alone and calls Ava Jones in LA.

"Okay Ava, it's all set, Michael will come over as soon as we land."

"What if he doesn't like me," says Ava, he may not vibe with me."

"You are one of the most beautiful Nubian woman that I have ever seen and you are definitely Michaels type, don't worry about that, just make sure you get him on tape. I need him having sex with you on tape. Are the cameras and recording equipment in place?"

"Yes, everything is set," says Ava, I just need Michael to take the bait and if he doesn't I have some enticement to slip in his drink. What about my money?"

"It's already in your account bitch," says Correta. "You know how I do business, just don't let me down."

" I got you," says Ava, if he is as horny as you say he is, it will be like taking candy from a baby." Coretta and Ava hang up and Cheryl walks into the isolated cabin.

"What are you up too," says Cheryl. "Looks like you're scheming again."

"Me," says Coretta sheepishly, what would give that idea?" Cheryl just stares at Coretta and walks back out of the cabin knowing Coretta is up to something. Cheryl walks past Michael's seat. "Don't you trust that woman," says Cheryl. "She's up to something." After Coretta's plane lands the rest of the entourage goes one way and Michael is whisked off for his meeting with Ava Jones. Inside Coretta's limo Cheryl is suspicious of the situation. She watches as Michael gets into a separate Limo away from the rest of the crew. "Where is Michael going," asks Cheryl to Coretta. "He said he had some business to take care of," says Correta. "A man gotta do what a man's gotta do."

"Really," says Cheryl. "Did you have anything to do with his plans?"

"Of course not," says Coretta, ` he had business to take care of, I just helped him out".

"Yeah I bet you did help him out," says Cheryl. With all that man has been through and what he still has to go through, I hope you are not setting him up for a fall."

"Why Cheryl," says Coretta," you think too little of me. He had something he needed to take care of and I just provided the means."

"Yeah I'll bet you did," says Cheryl. "Woman you'll never change." Cheryl just scowls at Coretta and sits back in her seat.

As soon as Michael gets into the other Limo he falls asleep and after a twenty minute ride they arrive at Ava Jones suite. Coretta's Limo driver wakes Michael up from his slumber to let him know that he has arrived at his destination.

"Mr. Alexander," says the driver, we are here sir, are you ok?" Michael jumps up as if he was having a nightmare and realizes where he is.

"Mr. Alexander this is the suite number and just go in and ride the elevator to the 10th floor," says the driver, Ms. Jones is in Suite 1035 and she is expecting you. You can phone Ms. James when you are ready to leave and I will pick you up."

"She said I only had to be here an hour," says Michael," and that's all I'm doing."

"That's totally up to you sir," says the driver," enjoy your evening." With that Michael exits the Limo and enters the luxurious plaza to the condos and rides the elevator upstairs. Everything is first class in the building including the elevator which is all glass and which moves up real fast almost like a ride at an amusement park. Michael exits the elevator and signs point that room 1035 is to the left. As he reaches the room Michael is not sure what to expect knowing Coretta. Inside the beautiful Ava Jones has her camera equipment and the room has rose petals leading to her bedroom and she is wearing an ultrashort pink short set with furry slippers on. Michael rings the doorbell and the gorgeous 5ft 7 inch Ava answers the door and immediately she makes eye contact with Michael and sparks fly on both sides.

"Mr. Alexander I presume," says Ava, I expected you to be enticing but sir you take my breath away."

"Ms. Jones," says Michael as he grabs her hand and kisses it,"the pleasure is all mine beautiful." "Would you have a seat sir," says Ava.

"Thank you," says Michael. Ava's suite has very beautiful white furnishing and Cherry Wood tables as Michael sits on the beautiful white loveseat Ava sits right next to him. What started off as a job for Ava turns into a pleasure and Michael for his part is equally enticed by the caramel skin of Ava Jones. Michael looks for flaws on the woman's body but see none, for she is beautiful from head to toe, very soft to the touch and she is to Michael very ladylike. Ava sees Michael as her dream come true and instead of just the usual lust they both find an unexpected passion and they just sit and talk for hours about their lives past and present. At about 2am Ava receives a text from Coretta, she has been so caught up in her conversation with Michael that she forgot her agreement.

"Is everything done," says Correta. "How was it girl."

"I'm still doing it, texts Ava back, will follow up with you in the morning. Coretta can't believe that Michael has been there for hours and is still there.

"Sorry about that," says Ava, Mr. Alexander it's getting late ,are you spending the night with me?" "Of course if that's ok?" says Michael.

"I wouldn't have it any other way. Do you mind if I take a shower first?"

"Not at all," says Ava, follow me sir." Ava takes Michael's hand and leads him to the shower and gets all the toiletries he needs and then turns on the shower. Michael steps into the shower and exhales as if a shower is what he needed all day. As Michael enjoys the water a nude Ava steps into the shower with him and the two kiss each other. Ava takes the wash cloth and lathers it and washes Michael's body from head to toe and in turn he does the same to her. Michael starts to kiss Ava's breasts and she enjoys his lips against her body and she in turn kisses all over him. The water splashing against their bodies makes it seem more erotic and Michael bends Ava over and sexes her in the shower and the pleasure of the moment is a lot more than Michael expected. After about ten minutes of pleasure the two leave the shower and dive into Ava's plush Queen size bed and continue their passionate love making with Michael not knowing that he is on candid camera.

"My legs are too long for this bed," says Michael while between Ava's legs, you need a bigger bed." We'll make it work," says Ava. At no time during the conversation do they stop loving each other. After a lot of passionate love Michael and Ava fall asleep and the next thing Michael knows it's 10 am and Ava is standing over him with waffles, eggs and juice.

"Wake up sleepy head," says Ava, sit up Michael." Ava props the pillow behind Michael's head and begins to feed him his waffles. Michael enjoys the moment and then realizes he has been out all night.

"What time is it?" asks Michael.

"It's 10:15am," says Ava. Michael jumps from the bed.

"I gotta go," says Michael. "I need to check on my family. Can I see you later?

"Of course," says Ava, here's my phone number, call me." Michael calls an Uber driver instead of calling Coretta and after 20 minutes the driver picks him at the front of the building. He gives Ava a big kiss goodbye and takes off. As soon as Michael leaves Coretta calls Ava.

"I've been waiting to hear from you," says Correta. "How did it go."

"It was wonderful," says an excited Ava,` `the best night of my life."

"You sound a little too excited," says Correta. "Get me the video immediately." Ava hesitates but she knows she can't back out of her arrangement with Coretta so she reluctantly agrees.

"Ok," says Ava and she immediately hangs up the phone. Coretta is a little puzzled at Ava's actions but glad her business is successful.

CHAPTER 44

THE PARTY

A few weeks later, Michael is throwing a large celebration at his house and all his friends are invited. About 100 people occupy the house including an old flame Myra Irvin who is there looking like a million dollars in a fitted pink dress. Eric stands near Michael and stares at Myra.

"That girl got body for days," says Eric, do you know her."

"Yea we've met before," says Michael. "She's a friend from way back." Michael's friend Steve is there and happy for Michael.

"Man I watched that shit unfold on TV and I still can't believe it, fucking identical twin, that's the kind of shit you only see in the movies. Man you should write a book and call it The Black Gigolo." "Man that shit won't sell," says Michael. Michael's daughter Brittany is at the party as he has brought her back to LA to be with him.

"Daddy I'm hungry," says Brittany to her father, can I eat."

"Baby this is your house," says Michael. "You can eat whenever you want. Go to the food table and get whatever you want."

"I'll get it for her," says Myra from a distance. She grabs Brittany's hand and leads her to the food. Donald stands close by and just admires all the sites coming in the place. Cheryl is across the way and comes over to Michael wearing a black dress that is almost too short to cover anything and she walks up and kisses Michael in front of everyone. "I want to thank you for standing by me," says Michael. "If you didn't believe in me I would not be here today."

"I love you Michael," says Cheryl. "And I always will. What's going to happen with your mom."

"She is in rehab," says Michael. "She is hanging in there but sometimes she doesn't know where she is. They say she blocked the trauma out of her mind. I'm there for her."

'You're a good son Michael," says Cheryl. "And how are you."

"I'm as good as I can be," says Michael. "I'll survive." Cheryl acknowledges his statement and walks off and Donald speaks.

"Don't bend over girl in that short ass dress," says Donald, cause we'll be able to see your whole future."

"Shut up Donald," says Cheryl as Michael and Eric laugh. As the people enjoy themselves a little boy is running around the party being mischievous and he runs up and kicks Michael on his leg out of nowhere.

"AW," yells Michael as the little boy laughs.

"Pooh Bear, yells his mother, behave yourself."

"Pooh bear, yells Michael, you should call that little fucker Grizzly Bear. Boy you lucky times have changed cause if I could I would get a switch and whip your little ass."

"You don't talk to kids like that," says the boys mother, come on Pooh Bear let's go."

"Yeah take his little bad ass home" says Michael. Across the way an uninvited guest is in the house.

"Isn't that your nosy ass neighbor Mrs. Crabbs?" asks Eric. "What is she doing here?"

"Hell if I know," says Michael as Mrs. Crabbs approaches wearing a white dress.

"Michael," says Mrs. Crabbs. "I'm so glad you are back. And I just want you to know that I always believed in you and I knew you wouldn't do that kind of stuff." Michael just frowns and Donald walks up behind Mrs. Crabbs with the punch bowl and pours it over her head.

"Oops," says Donald, but that red looks good on that white dress." Everyone at the party laughs and Mrs. Crabbs runs out the door screaming and dripping punch all over the floor.

"Mrs. Crabbs, that's a nice red and white dress you're wearing," says Donald, I'm gonna get my girl one."

"If your little short ass had a girl," says Cheryl. "Your right hand doesn't count."

"Left hand for me," says Donald, left hand." Michael looks up and walking in his house is a white man and woman that he has never seen before. Cheryl walks over to Michael.

"That's the new DA for LA County," says Cheryl. "After it came out that the last DA withheld your fingerprint evidence they probably went out of their way to come to your party. Probably scared you gonna sue their ass." The DA approaches Michael.

"I'm David Johnson of the Los Angeles County district Attorney's office and I wanted to come out and personally apologize for the actions of the last DA, withholding evidence is a serious offense," says David Johnson not calling the last DA's name, and oh, this my wife Donna." Donna is a heavy set white woman and very unattractive to Michael.

"We are happy that everything worked out well for you sir," says David Johnson, I'm not a fan of Gigolos I must admit, I know how I would feel if I came home and caught you in bed with my wife, I would feel like I'm dead." Michael looks at the man's wife.

"Look sir," says Michael. "The only way you would catch me in bed with your ugly ass wife is if I was already dead." Mr. Johnson's wife moves her husband to the side and walks up and faces Michael and speaks slowly.

"Who are you calling ugly?" asks Mrs. Johnson.

"You," says Michael. "I've seen cuter Gorillas." "You're the DA of Los County and you're going to stand there and let that man talk to your wife like that," Mrs. Johnson says to her husband, grow some balls man."

"Come on honey let's get some food," says the DA.

"There's some bananas over there," says Donald.

Moments later Coretta comes in with a member of her security and holding hands with a little boy. The security person is the one who threatened Michael in the car and he walks up to Michael and asks if he can see him in the kitchen. Across the way Michael sees Officer Andrews at the party and Officer Andrews notices the two men walking towards the kitchen and follows. The Security guy walks up to Michael.

"Remember I told you what I would do after all this was over," says the security guy, well I just want to squash it, you've been through enough, an ass whupping won't help." The security guy walks off and Michael walks behind him and calls him,

"Hey," says Michael. As the security turns around Michael hits him with a crushing right hand and the man drops to the floor like a sack of potatoes.

"Don't you ever speak on my mother again you sucker," says Michael. "Have a good sleep." Officer Andrews comes over and looks at the man.

"You sucker punched him," says Officer Andrews, but he had it coming."

"All's fair in love and war," says Michael. "Beside, he's a black belt, I didn't want to go heads up with him. Can you drag him out the back." Officer Andrews carries the man out and Michael walks back in as if nothing has happened and approaches Coretta who has recently joined the party holding hands with a little boy that she tells everyone is her son.

"You know we've definitely had our battles," says Michael to Coretta, but you gave me your all and without you, well, I don't even want to imagine where I would be." Michael looks at the little handsome boy holding Coretta's hand.

"And who is this handsome young man?" asks Michael. "The ladies gonna be in trouble when you get a little older."

"Hi," says the little boy, my name is Mike.

"Hello," says Michael smiling, and how old are you."

"I'm five," says the little boy," it's nice to meet you."

"Mike James," says Michael. "That's a smooth name."

"No silly," says the little boy, my name is Mike Alexander." Michael stops and looks at Coretta.

"Why would you name your son after me?" asks Michael.

"I'm sorry," says Correta. "Michael Alexander, meet Michael Alexander Jr. He's your son Michael." "What," says Michael. "That was six years ago and we did it one time," says Michael.

"One time is all it takes Michael," says Correta. "I wasn't gonna tell you but after I saw what happened with you and your brother I couldn't deny you or him the truth any longer." Michael just looks at the boy as Cheryl gasps and others stare.

"That's why she disappeared for all those years," says Myra Irvin, she was taking care of her child." "That also explains why she went to such lengths to help Michael, and he does look Michael, a lot like Michael" says Cheryl. Michael just hugs the boy and takes him over to meet his daughter Brittany as Coretta smiles and looks on.

"Two Michael Alexanders," says Donald, is the world ready. That would be almost as bad as two Donald's."

"You put two Donald's together and you still won't be tall enough to be one man," says Cheryl. "You can sit on a dime and swing your legs."

"You know you want some of this Cheryl," says Donald. The gesture makes Coretta James almost seem human and Michael is happy because he just lost a brother but he gained a son. Michael sobs a little and heads towards one of the bathrooms to wash his face and Myra notices and beats him to the bathroom and as Michael walks in and Myra has dropped her dress on the floor and stands there only in her birthday suit as Michael walks in the bathroom.

"Remember this Michael," says a nude Myra, it's been a long time." Michael looks at Myra hard.

"How can I forget that," says Michael. "But this is not the time or place." As Michael talks to a naked Myra Donald walks in.

"Oh my God," says Donald, I done died and gone to heaven, damn girl you fine as hell."

"Myra," says Michael. "Put your clothes on, I'm not going to do this with my children in the other room."

"You've changed Michael," says Myra," you would do it anytime, anywhere."

"Not anymore," says Michael as he walks out of the bathroom.

"I'll take his place," says Donald, let me show you what a real man can do."

"No thanks," says Myra while putting her dress back on. Right after that Donald emerges from the bathroom and talks to Michael.

"Michael I've been knowing you for many years," says Donald, and I've never seen you turn down a fine ass woman like that, what gives?"

"Donald, my friend, all my life I've been thinking with my little head," says Michael. "That's the only way my brother was able to use my life against me was because I gave him the ammunition. I've got a 10 year old and a 5 year old now, it's time for a change. Now if you don't mind brother I'm going over here and get to know my son." Donald just acknowledges Michael as Myra emerges from the bathroom.

"That offer still stands Myra," says Donald, the only way to truly have a fix is to mess with a man that is 5 foot six." Myra doesn't acknowledge Donald.

As Michael goes over to the other side of the room the doorbell rings and since Coretta is close by she opens the door.

"I'm sorry Michael for ringing the doorbell but I forgot my key," says the voice bending over to pick up her purse. As the woman stands up Coretta is shocked.

"Ava," says Correta. "I must say I'm surprised to see you." "Likewise," says Ava, I didn't know you were invited."

"I wasn't," says Correta. "I heard about it through the grapevine, Coretta James doesn't need an invitation."

"Of course not," says Ava.

"Ava, yells Brittany, it's so good to see you."

"It's good to see you honey," says Ava, look what I got you." Ava has brought Brittany a new doll to add to her doll collection.

"Oh thank you Ava," says Brittany, I'm going to put it with the rest." Cheryl, Myra and Coretta look on in amazement as Michael has started a new life that doesn't include them.

"Ava can I speak to you a moment alone," says Coretta. Michael greets Ava and kisses her in front of everyone and Ava excuses herself and walks in the kitchen to talk to Coretta.

"Are you living here with Michael," asks Coretta, I just needed you to do a job for me, I didn't expect you to shack up with him."

"I love that man Coretta," says Ava, "I loved him from the moment I saw him, and I believe he loves me too." As Coretta and Ava talk Cheryl eves drops on their conversation. As they talk Michael walks into the kitchen with his new son that he shares with Coretta and introduces him to Ava.

"Ava," says Michael. "This is Mike, Michael Jr., my son with Coretta. I just met him today". Ava stares at Coretta and then kneels down and introduces herself to little Mike.

"Hello Michael," says Ava, "it's very nice to meet you."

"Hello," says Mike, "are you my daddy's wife?"

"No," says Ava," but your dad and I are very close and I look forward to getting to know you too. Michael you didn't tell me you had a son." Michael doesn't want to talk in front of little Mike.

"Come on Mike let's get that drink you want," says Michael. "We will talk later baby." Michael kisses Ava and after he retrieves a drink for little Mike he leaves the women to talk.

"You and Michael have a son," says Ava, "is that why you wanted that video so bad?'

"Got to protect my interests," says Correta. "In case he tries to take my son I will always have leverage. You see Ava, Michael is a hoe, always has been and he always will be and there's nothing you can do about it. The dick can't be that good to make you fall head over heels so quickly, you will never be number one in Michael's life." "It's not about the dick," says Ava, " yes he is good to me physically but that's because he's good to me mentally and every other way. Michael is special, he is not just a "hoe" as you say. Michael is a man, a man in every way and he makes me feel like a woman in every way and that's something you would never understand." As Ava says that she exits the kitchen.

"I'm going to tell Michael what you did to him," yells Coretta as Ava opens the kitchen door and others at the party hear her yell and look around. Ava walks back and approaches Coretta.

"I already told him," says Ava, and he wants to see the video himself. Michael wants to check out his moves". Ava snickers at Coretta as she leaves the kitchen. Coretta walks out and all eyes are on her as she steps back into the party. As Ava walks by Cheryl, Cheryl asks her a question.

"Why did you give Coretta the video," says an eavesdropping Cheryl, you could have just destroyed it." Ava approaches Cheryl.

"That's Coretta James," says Ava," they might have found me at the bottom of the ocean."

"And how do you know she won't try something now," asks Cheryl.

"I don't care anymore," says Ava, I'm happy now and I don't fear Coretta James or anyone else." Ava walks up to Michael.

"Honey, I'm going in the room to take a shower," says Ava kissing Michael and she walks off to their bedroom with several eyes on her. As soon as Michael kisses Ava he stares at the door and sees the last person he expects, Bones from the Gang party. Michael approaches him.

"I've followed your story on the news," says Bones. "You can't make that stuff up."

"You strapped?" asks Michael.

"No I left it in the car," says Bones. "Michael you really touched me that night and my real name is Richard Reese, not Bones."

"Well come and meet my family Rich," says Michael.

CHAPTER 45

At about 1 am the party has started winding down, Brittany and her new brother little Mike are fast asleep and the last few people are leaving and Donald is of course spending the night.

"Good night Michael," says a disappointed Myra, "hopefully I can see you soon."

"Call me baby," says Michael as he kisses Myra, "we need to talk."

"Let me know if you need anything," says Cheryl as she exits, "I'm available 24\7.Congratulations on your new son. You're gonna do DNA just to make sure he's yours?"

"That's already been done, thank you," says Correta. "Standing by, "I guess you think I was born under a rock. I was born at night, but not last night. I knew he was going need proof. Now go home and enjoy that empty bed of yours." Cheryl just gives Coretta another look and leaves.

"I'm trusting you with my son tonight," says Coretta as she leaves, make sure my baby is safe."

"Our baby right," says Michael. "Don't worry, I got him."

"Okay," says Correta. "Our baby, I'll call in the morning, tell Ava I said goodnight," adds Coretta sarcastically.

Coretta leaves and Donald is still drinking and a "buzzed" Michael looks in on his children and they are both sleeping peacefully and Michael goes to his room and he sees that Ava is sleeping peacefully and rather than wake her he goes to the sofa to watch sports out front. Michael looks at a text from Ken.

"I dropped that body guard off into Coretta's Limo, texts Ken, he's Probably woke by now." Michael snickers and falls asleep on the sofa. At about 3am that same morning Michael feels something "poking" him in his face and he believes he is dreaming. As he finally opens his eyes he sees a .357 magnum pointed at him with the hammer already cocked which means it can possibly go off at the slightest touch. Standing over him is a woman he recognizes, Lieutenant Jocelyn Towns from the Sherman Oaks Police department.

"Get your ass up," says Lieutenant Towns. "This is for all the women you have ever used."

"Towns what the fuck is wrong with you," says Michael. "How did you get in this house?"

"I just came through the front door while the party was going on," says Lieutenant Towns. "I just hid in one of the rooms. Can't believe nobody noticed me, having too much fun I guess. Not get your raping ass up, let's do this outside, we'll try not to wake those beautiful children."

"Towns I didn't rape anybody, you know that," says Michael. "It was my brother, what are you doing this for."

"It might have been your brother," says Towns. "But you are just as responsible as he is. The man who molested my sister got away. Darlene Orbison will never be the same for the rest of her life, and there are many others out there like her. Somebody needs to pay and I choose you. Besides, I don't like your smart ass anyway."

"Why, because I won't give your ugly ass no dick."

"Keep running your mouth and you're gonna get shot inside," says Lieutenant Towns. "Hurry up, open that door."

Michael opens the front door and the sound of the alarm when the door opens wakes a drunken Donald who falls off the guest room couch onto the floor.

"Shit that hurts," says Donald, when notices the open door. Outside Lieutenant Towns is about to execute Michael.

"Get on your knees, yells Lieutenant Towns, I want to see your ass beg."

"Never," says Michael. "You're going to have to shoot me like this, I only bow down to God." Lieutenant Towns starts to pull the trigger when the front door burst open and as she looks back Donald hits her across her head with the iron from the fireplace knocking her unconscious and the gun goes off in the direction of the side of the house and the loud sound wakes a few neighbors including Mrs. Crabb who immediately calls the police. Michael and Donald are not sure where the bullet went but no one around them is hurt. Ava runs out the front door and puts her arms around Michael.

"I'm fine baby," says Michael. Ava stares at Lieutenant Towns lying on the ground and she sees the gun and she breathes a sigh of relief. "Where the fuck did she come from?" asks Donald. "That shit was close."

"She was hiding somewhere in the house," says Michael. "That's the crazy ass Lieutenant that has been harassing me every since this case started, she was obsessed with me and this case. Brother you saved my ass again. I'm going to check on the kids, you stay out here and wait for the police. You know that nosy ass Mrs. Crabbs already called them. Why don't you go over there and give old ass Mrs Crabbs some loving."

"Hell no," says Donald, that's even below my standards." Even Ava laughs.

Meanwhile as Michael finds his way out of another calamity in Los Angeles, over in Annecy, France a suburb of Paris a woman readies herself for a night out on the town as her escort knocks on the door. The man speaks French.

"Bonsoir madame je suis votre rendez-vous de la soirée,"says the man.(Good evening Ma'am I am your date for the evening)

"Bien bonne soirée," says the woman, tu es un sil bel homme."(Well good evening sir, you are such a handsome man.)

"Et puis-je demander comment vous-appelez vous?"(And may I ask what is you name)

"Mon nom est Michel Alexander," says the man.
(MY NAME IS MICHAEL ALEXANDER)

THE END

CPSIA information can be obtained
at www.ICGtesting.com
Printed in the USA
LVHW032131040921
696921LV00002B/2